KAMYONISTAN REVISITED

KAMYONISTAN REVISITED

ROBERT HACKFORD

ATHENA PRESS
LONDON

KAMYONISTAN REVISITED
Copyright © Robert Hackford 2008

All Rights Reserved

ISBN: 978 1 84748 434 5

First published 2008 by
ATHENA PRESS
Queen's House, 2 Holly Road
Twickenham TW1 4EG
United Kingdom

Printed for Athena Press

Azhar

Bingo, a British lorry driver nearing retirement, descended the mountain road that led to Damascus. His brakes were hot, even though he had endeavoured to use his exhaust-brake all the way down; his face was hot, even though the windows were open; and the seat was hot, even though he kept lifting one buttock then the other for ventilation. The external sun visor above his windscreen dipped below the line of hazy hills ahead and sunlight splashed the glass with greasy gold. Steering his heavily laden DAF off the main road onto a narrow lane, he followed the familiar route to Kamyonistan. Passing under the imposing Islamic archway at its entrance, he entered the truck stop and lurched over its dusty, uneven ground in low gear. After carefully parking with the back of the trailer facing the sun, he and his passenger locked the cab and made their way to the drivers' restaurant, where they ordered *shay* and sat out on the veranda. From here they could watch the coming and going of lorries against a backdrop of mountains spiked with the creamy minarets and dusty palms of Kamyonistan.

That was the afternoon Amoun had a baby – not in the bio-logical sense, because fifteen-year-old boys can't have babies. He acquired the tiny sliver of humanity when it appeared that one of the other boys, also fifteen, had died in childbirth. Amoun had been trying for months to escape from the Syrian truck stop known as Kamyonistan. He was gifted at stowing away in lorries bound for Turkey and Europe, but he suffered from confidence-shattering ill luck when it came to passing out of the transport zone undetected by the police or the customs officials who checked the lorries, especially those that had loaded on the site.

Amoun, a Palestinian runaway, preferred to work alone, and he had turned his hand to anything he could in order to feed himself. His customers were drivers whose trucks he polished, or for whom he ran errands. In recent weeks, however, there had been a new influx of Palestinian refugees from Lebanon. Most of them were in their teens and Amoun had been drawn into a network of mutual support. In spite of his slight build, the new boys had looked to Amoun for leadership, not least because he had been living rough in Kamyonistan for over a year and he knew the ropes.

One of the boys, Salah, had been slightly odd, to Amoun's mind. He hadn't played football in quite the same way as the others. Also, he'd had a very strange attitude to ablutions and toilet, which had rather isolated him because he was so fiercely private about it all. There was something disconcertingly unmanly about him.

That afternoon, the air was hot and still. A haze lay over Kamyonistan, veiling the mountains and turning the light yellow. A piercing scream drew half a dozen refugee boys running to an abandoned trailer, parked against the high wall. Salah's trousers were at half mast and he was lying on his back. He seemed to be emitting a high-pitched shriek. Ducking under the trailer chassis, the boys crouched over Salah. There was a sudden quietness in the thick bar of shadow beneath the wagon. His thighs and torso were covered in blood.

'He's killed himself!' Amoun said.

'Wait! Feel his pulse.'

'See if he's breathing.'

'He's been stabbed, look!'

'Ugh! What's that horrible thing on his front?' Then the screaming started again, but it was coming from the horrible thing on his front.

'It's Shaitan! Run!'

'No, it's an animal. It's killed Salah. It'll get us too.'

'Don't be stupid – it's a baby!'

'How did a baby get there?' Amoun picked up the slimy creature and turned it in his hands, instinctively supporting its little head. 'It's still attached,' he said. 'Quick, get that small water bottle out of my pocket. I'll wash it.' He began to bathe the howling infant.

'Look!' one of them shouted. 'Salah hasn't got a dick! He's a girl!'

'She's not breathing,' said the older boy, pulling out his knife. 'We'll have to cut the cord.' He hesitated. 'This isn't my thing,' he said. Then he fainted.

Other boys tried to bring him round. Someone attempted to revive the girl.

'Give her the kiss of life,' one of them suggested.

'I'm going to save the baby,' Amoun said, decisively. Seizing the big boy's knife, he sliced the umbilical cord, tied a knot near the baby end and re-washed his tiny charge. Then he wrapped him – for it was a boy – in his *shamagh* and cradled him in his arms. The bigger boy, whose name was Hamid, recovered and tried to revive the girl, but with no success.

'She can't be all that dead,' protested one boy. 'Didn't you hear her screaming?'

'That was the baby,' Amoun said. 'I don't think Salah – the girl, I mean, did any screaming at all.'

'She was probably dead before we got here, then,' said Hamid glumly.

They sat there, the young refugees, in the dust of the sultry afternoon. A muezzin's call to prayer filled the air with its waves of sound and the boys looked at each other; Amoun cradling the groggy infant, the big boy sitting cross-legged with the dead girl's head in his lap, one wide-eyed youngster staring into the space between her legs with his hands covering his mouth, another kneeling with Amoun's water bottle in one hand. When the sound of the mosque's chant had subsided, the boy holding the water murmured, 'What shall we do?' They all knew that this was an impossible situation. Not because anyone believed that a boy had given birth, but because they were all outlaws. If they went to the authorities, there might be big trouble.

'They'll think we murdered her,' Hamid declared.

'They'll think we got her pregnant,' said another.

'We'll have to bury her.'

'We can't do that. We'll have to hand her over.'

'The baby'll die without milk.'

'We can buy that or get it from Mehmet in the restaurant.'

'No,' Amoun said, firmly. 'He has to have real breast milk or he'll die.'

No one spoke for some minutes. The baby stirred in Amoun's arms. He said, 'I think we should take the baby to Mehmet and ask him what to do. He helps us sometimes.'

Mehmet was the jovial and sympathetic manager of the drivers' restaurant. It was called the Paradise Restaurant and Amoun was well known in there. Hamid looked alarmed. 'Wait!' he said. 'The girl! We can't just go in there leaving a body under the trailer. They won't believe us if we tell them the truth.'

'They will,' Amoun said. 'A doctor would know straight away that she died in childbirth.'

A curious little huddle of boys presented themselves at the counter in the restaurant. It was too early for many customers and the few drivers who had gone in for *shay* were smoking on the veranda outside. Mehmet looked momentarily alarmed, until he spotted Amoun among the lads. Amoun explained about the baby, then about the corpse. Mehmet frowned. 'We'll have to tell the police,' he said. 'But I'll help you.'

At that moment, Mahmout, who ran his father's truck-wash business, breezed in. Mehmet spoke urgently with him; then he turned to Amoun. 'You're lucky, and so is this little fellow,' he said. 'Go with Mahmout. His cousin's friend is producing more milk than her own baby can drink, so she may feed this child. I doubt if she'll take him in, though.'

So it was that Amoun became a surrogate father. The kind and copious lactator agreed to feed the baby every four hours on condition that Amoun presented him clean and properly looked after. Otherwise, responsibility for him was entirely Amoun's. The few families who lived on the edge of the truck stop were poor and had mouths enough to feed. Mehmet promised to try and get one of the orphanages in Damascus to adopt him, but said that without documents this would not be easy. That evening the police questioned the boys about the body, which they had earlier sent away in an ambulance.

Amoun felt sad that the little mite had lost its mother, and sadder still that its mother had probably been running from certain death at the hands of her own family, having dishonoured them with a pregnancy that in all likelihood had been forced upon her by one of them...

Amoun carried the little bundle wherever he went. He was sensitive to the needs of his baby and took his responsibilities very seriously indeed. As a strictly temporary measure, Mehmet let Amoun sleep in an outhouse behind the restaurant so that he could have access to sanitation. In an attempt to fudge his identity a little, Amoun habitually wore the brown and white Arab-pattern *shamagh* favoured in parts of Sinai. In reality, it identified him quite strongly as a boy who wore the only brown *shamagh* in Kamyonistan, probably the only one in Damascus and possibly the only one in Syria. Now, he used it to swaddle the newborn baby, its colours proving useful in camouflaging evidence of infant waste. Amoun named him Azhar, which meant 'radiant'. Already, he loved this tiny manifestation of Allah's high regard for the world in general and Kamyonistan in particular.

Cairo to Kamyonistan

On the coast of the Gulf of Aquaba in a little port town called Nuweiba, two boys were washing trucks in the brilliant sunlight. To protect their heads from Egypt's sun, they covered their heads with *shamaghs*. Ro, an English boy, and Nuri, an Egyptian Beduin, had met in the Kamyonistan truck stop when they were still fifteen and had caused a stir by operating a camel-aided truck wash and by falling in love with each other. Now, at sixteen, they were continuing their business on the palm-lined road into the port, where lorries queued to board the ferries to Jordan. They lived in a tiny abandoned hut on the edge of town. Here, they tended the two camels and lived largely in the open. For several weeks they had led a pleasant existence, washing lorries for friendly Arab drivers, chatting in the bustling cafés among the shipping offices opposite the port or just lounging on Nuweiba's beautiful beaches. The previous week the two boys had taken the camels far into the wild mountains that formed a dramatic backdrop to the town, sleeping in blankets under the stars and cooking over acacia wood fires. High in the wilderness they had found a magic place sheltered on three sides, the back wall of which contained a spring with palm trees on either side. Here, they had been content to exist in the timeless silence. Ro had named it 'Ain Nuri, but Nuri told him that there was a Beduin name for it, which he had forgotten.

Whenever they could, the boys put in an appearance at the mosque. This reassured those who were perplexed by Ro's presence. Ro looked forward to the quiet sanctity of the place, though he disliked the imam's hectoring at Friday prayers. Ro's reservations about Islam were political rather than religious. He had been attracted to Islam as a religion and had recognised in it the kind of spirituality that suited him. In many ways the beauty of Islam as a religion made it the most beguiling spiritual route of all. Unfortunately, Islam's political aspects were inseparable from its spiritual ones. This frustrated and saddened him greatly. He knew that in most religions, his relationship with God could be private and relatively uncontaminated by wider politics. If he embraced the lovely, clean lines of spiritual Islam, however, he would be forced to accept the unlovely, jagged lines of political Islam featuring the possibilities of physical mutilations and capital punishments embedded in medieval justice systems; the imposition of tyrants as leaders in some places; the constant, judgemental censorship of one Muslim for another on the streets; and an institution that failed to recognise the innocence of same-sex love. It seemed to Ro that a perfectly good religion had cluttered itself with some very unattractive, negative trappings that would surely, in the long run, erode its strength from within.

Notwithstanding this catalogue of perceived shortcomings, Islam still drew Ro to it, and he had fallen into the routine habits of daily ritual ablution and prayer, along with Nuri. In some ways, this apparent devotion gave them protection from possible hostility. It made the *khawaga* kid less visible and blurred the implications of the boys' relationship. Their frequent appearance in the mosque was always pronounced by the presence, outside, of their tethered camels. One evening the imam suggested that Ro's conversion should be formalised. To this end, the following evening, Ro took a symbolic shower in the mosque to cleanse him of other spiritual influences, before joining the gathered port workers for prayers. It was a powerful and beautiful ritual, and a memorable occasion for Ro. He was given a Muslim name to use as he saw fit. The men and boys embraced him, murmuring, '*Mash'allah* – it is God's will,' before sharing a meal with him in the mosque courtyard. Their generosity of spirit warmed him.

The following week, a lorry left Egypt's capital for the Levant. Even though Wahid was a regular driver on the Amman to Cairo run, he was never happy with any load that took him any nearer to the great, sprawling Arab city of Cairo than its ring road. On this occasion, however, he had delivered equipment to a police station in the heart of an ancient part of the city built during the tenth to fourteenth centuries and known loosely as Fatimid Cairo.

Heavy lorries were discouraged in its tight lanes, but as this had been a government job, Wahid had received a police escort. Now empty, he wove through the early morning traffic in smoky streets where the long shadows of decorated minarets alternated with yellow bands of misty light. The police escort was making little difference to progress, but his presence would be useful if things jammed up too badly. Easing his MAN 19.321 among the horse-drawn market wagons laden with garlic and okra, Wahid changed up a gear in the Fuller Road-Ranger box and moved out of a narrow street into the Midan Salah ad-Din, where a magnificent crowd of tall mosques greeted him. Lush palm trees stood green against their shadows, and high above them the minarets of Muhammad Ali mosque stood dramatically upon the hill. Watching his trailer wheels in the mirror, the Jordanian negotiated the big roundabout and straightened up, dodging sleek BMWs and taxis to find the exit.

When the police car left him to fend for himself, he went to an industrial location further out of town to pick up his return load. The building materials were waiting in a yard alongside the River Nile, where dusty palms and willows dragged in the water. Here, he sipped *shay* while the sun rose high and his trailer was loaded. Receiving the paperwork, Wahid checked and double-checked it before setting out for Kamyonistan. If he made good progress, he would arrive in Nuweiba about ten hours later, where he would have to queue for the ferry to Aquaba.

The road to Suez was busy and there were queues to go through the tunnel under the shipping canal. After that, Wahid made his way along the battered road that ran across the Sinai desert to Nakhl, meaning 'palm', where he stopped at a roadside truck stop near the mosque. In the unrelenting heat, Wahid ordered *shay* and a kebab sandwich while he flicked his hand at the flies. After a brief catnap, he drove into the evening. Slowly, in low gear, Wahid crawled down the steep mountain road that connected the desert plateau to the Red Sea coast at Taba on the Israeli border. Here, he underwent police checks and searches, even though he was only skirting the border and not crossing it. Finally, with constant mesh clunk, he put the MAN in gear again and drove the last leg of his day's journey to Nuweiba, where he joined the end of the long queue of trucks waiting to enter the port.

The following day, Ro and Nuri were washing the Jordanian MAN, chatting while they worked. Their camels stood in the paved central reservation, bearing canisters of water and spare brushes. 'I'm still surprised you became a Muslim,' Nuri said pausing, rag in hand. 'You know, after all you have said about Islam and our love for each other.'

'This way I'll learn more about why people think we're wrong. Maybe they aren't interpreting the Hadith correctly,' Ro answered. 'But I know what you mean. Gay Islam is not about to catch on in a big way, is it?'

'I'm glad you did it though,' Nuri said reassuringly. He passed Ro his long-handled brush so that he could reach the high part of the truck's cab. Having only one arm as a result of being struck by lightning, Nuri generally confined himself to the lower panels.

A bearded, scholarly looking man in a skullcap and a faun jalabiya stopped and greeted the boys in a rather formal manner. They recognised him from the mosque. He spoke earnestly in Arabic with Nuri, who then turned to Ro. 'He wants to know when you had the snip,' Nuri said, squinting into the sun. Ro hesitated.

'Oh, I can't remember,' he said.

'But you're not circumnavigated at all!' Nuri whispered.

'Circum*cised*,' Ro corrected. 'Just tell him it was too long ago to remember, as if it's any of his business.'

The man looked dubious when Nuri relayed this information to him: Nuri was not a good liar. When the cleric had gone, Nuri said, 'You'll have to have it done one day, now that you're a Muslim.'

'Absolutely not!' Ro replied, tartly. 'This is how Allah made me. My foreskin has served me perfectly well without any problems whatsoever for sixteen years and it's not for me or any arrogant cleric to improve on his design.'

'But all Muslims have to get it done!' protested Nuri.

'I don't care,' Ro said firmly. 'I think it's totally unnecessary genital mutilation. I appreciate that some people have to be circumcised for medical reasons or because their nozzles are a bit too tight; but apart from that I reckon it's just an excuse to sabotage sexual pleasure. It's an underhand plot to ruin a boy's sexual expression, using hygiene as a feeble excuse.' He handed the brush back to Nuri. They threw handfuls of water up the side of the cab.

The driver appeared and opened a big locker mounted on the chassis of the trailer. Pulling out some Turkish stools and a gas burner, he began to prepare *shay*. Nuri shuffled and adjusted his *shamagh*, for the sun was right overhead. 'Ro, if you're going to be a Muslim, you can't just pick and choose the bits you like,' he said.

'Why not? Isn't that the whole point of religion – that you take what you can from it and make it work for you so that you can become a better person?'

'Islam sort of isn't like that. You can't just dip into it. It's a whole system to which you become entirely committed.'

'That's good, coming from a gay Muslim!' Ro retorted.

'I've always been a Muslim; I have to make the best of what already is,' Nuri stated.

'Well, I'm going to start with the bits I like and can understand. Anyway, when do they ever check whether you've been done or not?' Ro demanded.

'When you get married, of course!' Nuri said and began to laugh.

'Exactly. Since I'm never likely to get married, no one is ever going to worry about it,' Ro said. Nuri looked relieved. The Jordanian driver called the boys over and the three of them sat down to drink *shay* in the shade of the trailer, where a flock of little brown goats jostled and foraged at their feet.

Ro thanked the driver and in his sparse, halting Arabic he asked him where he had loaded. 'Cairo,' replied Wahid, the driver. 'I am taking this load to Syria.'

'Damascus?' Ro inquired.

'Nearby; north of Damascus.'

'On the way to Homs?'

'Yes. It's a little place, a transport zone where the mountains start.'

'Kamyonistan?' Nuri asked, sitting upright.

'Yes!' the driver replied, surprised. 'You know it?'

'We used to live there. We started our camel wash there, didn't we, Ro.'

'Of course!' the driver exclaimed. 'I remember hearing about you. You must have lunch with me. Another driver is bringing some more food with him in a few minutes.' So they prepared a meal and shared it among the persistent, shoving goats in the middle of the port road.

Five sat round the lowered lid of the trailer locker and pre-pared to tuck into a meal of rice, tuna, cheese, bread and olives. Ro uttered, 'Bismillah!' quietly before reaching for the bread.

The second driver's assistant looked up and said, 'You're a Muslim?' Ro nodded with his mouth full. '*Inta kwayyis* – you're good,' continued the assistant. Ro thanked him. The second driver added, 'Islam is very good. The perfect thing.'

Ro looked at him, hesitated and being Ro, he said, 'No, it's not. It's very good but it's not perfect.' Nuri shot him a look that said, 'You just don't know when to shut up, do you.'

'You can't say that! You must never, ever say that!' the assistant said, raising his voice. Nuri looked alarmed and Ro remembered poor Nuri's fear when he had dared to question Islam among the gang of youths in Kamyonistan. Ro, who was always happiest sailing close to the wind said, 'Islam is a collection of ideas – religious ideas and political ideas rolled into one – but ideas nonetheless.'

'What are you trying to say?' The voice came from behind them and they turned. It was the cleric. Ro had not realised that the cleric spoke any English. He thought for a moment and said, 'Well, no idea is above criticism, whether it's Christianity, atheism, communism, Islam or anything else. They are all there to be challenged, aren't they?'

'No,' replied the cleric curtly. 'Islam is already a mature, fully formed religion. It isn't for ignorant teenagers to question it.'

'Then how are ignorant teenagers to understand it? Teenagers don't do blind faith. Not where I come from. Do they here?' Ro replied a little petulantly adding, 'Surely, Islam's robust enough to stand a bit of scrutiny… isn't it?'

'I'll be watching you,' the cleric said. 'God punishes those who corrupt Muslims.'

'I can cope more easily with the wrath of God than I can with yours. He is compassionate. Are you?' The cleric stared at Ro with contempt, looked pityingly at Nuri, nodded at the drivers with pursed lips and swept away. Like a nineteenth-century curate, he still had the authority of the 'Church' on his side. Ro had grasped that, and quite enjoyed rebelling against it, but in doing so he always seemed to compromise Nuri's safety. It wasn't disregard for Nuri's safety so much as youthful unawareness of the possible consequences of his cavalier excursions into religious discourse that had anything to do with Islam. Nuri said, 'One of these days you're going to open your mouth and your brains will fall out!'

That evening, the air remained hot. Riding their camels along the silvering waters of the shoreline, they arrived at a quiet stretch of beach. Pulling off their jalabiyas, they slid into the pleasant ambience of the Red Sea and relaxed. Inland, the mountains rose dramatically in the gathering dusk. The little lights of passing ships could be seen against the far cliffs of Saudi Arabia. Ro lay back and kicked white froth without a care in the world, while Nuri paddled himself gently about with his one arm and tried to banish the nagging doubts he had about the growing tensions between Ro and the cleric. Ro drew alongside his friend and held his waist. 'What's up, mate?'

'When you came to Nuweiba, you promised me you'd be discreet,' Nuri said.

'I am,' Ro replied.

'No, you are drawing too much attention with your arguments about religion. If you upset people like the cleric, it won't be long before they start to look for excuses to make trouble, and they won't have far to look. It didn't take Tariq long to work out what we mean to each other in Kamyonistan. Here, it will be even easier.'

'I hate living a lie,' Ro said.

'Get used to it or we'll have to look for somewhere else to live,' Nuri said with uncharacteristic vehemence.

'I'll try.'

'Why don't you stop fighting Islam? Just trust it,' Nuri said.

Darkness fell around them like a warm, velvet cloak as they

led their beasts back along the beach. Nuri sang softly above the sighing sea. Ro remained deep in thought. Life on the Gulf of Aqaba was in some ways idyllic, but nonetheless fraught with the unfathomable complexities of existence in the Middle East.

Leading their camels between the parked lorries in the port road, after buying essential groceries, the boys were chatting amiably when an unlit police pickup approached at speed. It hit Nuri's camel, swerved and mounted the kerb. The camel lay still. Angrily, two policemen leaped out. The boys were taken into custody. Both of them were frightened because they knew only too well that Egyptian policemen needed little excuse to indulge in a little brutality. After his first few words of protest, Ro realised that it was futile to argue that the car was unlit and travelling too fast. Then it was pointed out that Ro's visa was out of date. He was asked for his work permit. Nuri began to explain that Ro was just helping out and that Nuri was the worker, but he was silenced harshly. The boys were detained in a bare room for a couple of hours. Nuri was convinced that they were not local policemen. Eventually, the driver of the police pickup returned.

'We will confiscate your other camel and let you go. You have three days to get your visa and a work permit. Then you must come back and report to us. If you don't come back, we will find you and imprison you,' he told them.

They were tired. Outside they could hear the good camel protesting as it was led into the yard of the station.

Returning to the port road, they could find little trace of Nuri's camel. A shout attracted their attention. It was Wahid, the driver of the Jordanian truck, who had fed them at midday. He was waving two plastic carrier bags. Nuri greeted him and asked where his camel was. 'It was dead. A police breakdown wagon removed it,' Wahid said. 'Look, I saved your groceries.' He handed them their bags.

Ro thanked him. He felt depressed about the loss of the camel. Also, he knew that he hadn't any chance of obtaining a work permit and he believed he would have to go to Cairo for a visa, which would only be valid for one month. Cairo was eight hours away by bus and he would have to find the fare. 'How long will it take you to get to Kamyonistan?' Ro asked.

'Two days, inshallah, depending on the ferry and the borders,' Wahid replied.

Ro turned to Nuri, who had become distressed about the camels. 'Let's go to Syria,' he said bluntly. Turning to the driver, he said, 'If you let us hide in your load, we'll say you didn't know anything about us if we're caught.' The driver frowned and hesitated. 'I could get into a lot of trouble if they don't believe you,' he said. 'Do you know what you're doing? Have you thought this plan through?'

Ro knew that they had not. He said, 'We'll be careful. We learned a lot about stowing away from the refugee kids when we lived in Kamyonistan. We've got our groceries here to live on. We'll be really careful, won't we, Nuri?'

Nuri was paying little attention. His grief was getting the better of him. Wahid told them to sit quietly in the shadow of the trailer until the road was quiet. In the darkness, he made a space deep in the load for the boys to hide in. The trailer was an open backed, high-sided, Arab-style affair with a mixed load of building materials. Finally, he handed them a blanket. It was the one from Nuri's camel. Ro wondered if the driver had originally intended to keep it. He fell asleep comforting Nuri.

The Meeting of Needs

Kamyonistan shimmered in the early mist. The sun was already hot, and it set aglow the creamy stone of the walls and soaring minarets that enclosed the truck stop in the style of a medieval caravanserai. In the stillness of a summer sunrise, it could almost have been one. Bingo's passenger was one of the first to stir that morning. The adventurous retired schoolteacher slipped from the lower bunk of the lorry and went to perform her ablutions before all those big, hairy, foreign truckers got to the shower block. Bingo had recently upgraded to a DAF 95 XF with a Super Space-cab and Titania Roberts was loath to relinquish her generous bed. The stones crunched beneath Titania's feet and sent tiny clouds of dust into the air. Most of the mist had cleared. A skylark sang high above her. As she passed a cluster of Syrian wagons, one of them burst into life, the driver having fired up the engine for the air conditioning. The last time Titania had been here was when she was on holiday with an overland tour group going to Khartoum. Then, she had become embroiled in the complex relationship between Bingo and the two teenagers, Ro and Nuri. This had resulted in her taking one of the boys, Ro, home to England. Now, she had come down with Bingo for the ride, the travel, the experience and the company, for she and Bingo had a good 'platonic' relationship.

Titania showered and changed undisturbed. At sixty, she wasn't expecting to be inundated with unwanted attention, but this was the Middle East, after all. On the way back to the DAF, she heard the incongruous sound of a newborn baby crying. Puzzled, she followed the sound to the trailer of a Jordanian truck. Propped against one of the huge trailer wheels was a young boy nursing a baby wrapped in a brown Arab-pattern *shamagh*. She crouched beside the boy. He squinted at her and said in English, 'Hello! You were here before.'

19

'Good heavens! Fancy you remembering me!' Titania exclaimed. She extended her hand and the boy shook it. 'Titania,' she said. '*Ismi Titania.*'

'*Ismi Amoun,*' Amoun said brightly.

'Is this your baby?' Titania asked.

'Yes, sort of. He's called Azhar. I thought of the name myself.'

'Try to keep his face out of the sun, Amoun. His eyes are very new and the sunlight could damage them.' Amoun frowned in momentary irritation; then overcoming his pride, he pulled the *shamagh* across to cast a shadow on Azhar's face. His growing love for the infant was manifesting itself more and more in Amoun's determination to meet the little soul's every need. Titania plonked herself down next to the unlikely pair and rested her back against a grubby wheel. With the sun warming her face, she listened in astonishment to Azhar's short life story. She asked Amoun how he was going to feed both himself and the baby. He hesitated before making an ambiguous remark about the generosity of drivers whose desires could simply be gratified.

Titania was no brainless do-gooder, but she rarely missed an opportunity to take a little responsibility for the smooth running of the world about her. She slipped him some change. 'While I'm here, I can help you to look after your baby,' she said smiling. Amoun scowled and held the baby away from her. 'I didn't say I'll look after the baby for you,' she added gently. 'I mean that I can teach you ways of keeping little Azhar healthy and happy. I won't take him from you.'

Amoun visibly relaxed and Azhar broke wind. Titania showed the teenager how to help the baby break wind comfortably, by putting him on Amoun's shoulder and encouraging him to pat the tiny back very gently.

When Titania reached the DAF, Bingo was checking the fluid levels before starting the engine. The kettle steamed away on its little stove in the trailer locker. Stools were set out and the wherewithal for an English breakfast lay arrayed on the locker lid, which served as a table.

'With any luck we'll get ourselves tipped today, then I can organise a back load,' Bingo said, wiping his hands on a rag. This truck stop served the transport zone in which Bingo hoped to unload his cargo. Usually, he brought cloth down and took ready-made garments back, but this time he had the furniture and household effects of someone who had taken a post in Damascus teaching English.

After breakfast, they ambled over to the freight agents' building. Bingo was requested to drive round to a warehouse in one of the neighbouring compounds, wait for customs to break the seals, open up the back of the trailer and reverse onto a loading bay indicated by the customs officer. 'This is very efficient!' Bingo commented. 'We could be in Spain or France. I wouldn't hold your breath if I were you, Tania, there's plenty that can hold us up yet!'

'Shall I come with you, or can I go and sit on the veranda and sip *shay*?'

'You sip *shay*,' Bingo said. 'Or instruct that youngster of yours in post-natal care.'

Bingo's truck left in a slow cloud of billowing dust. Titania walked through the haphazard arrangement of parked lorries in the direction of Restaurant Janna. A group of teenage boys kicking a deflated ball about on the rough surface of the compound caught her attention. She stood and watched their skinny forms darting happily under the sun and thought of the fat, well-fed kids who loitered sullenly with expensive music destroying their eardrums outside her house. The footballers called to one another with sounds that communicated affection and nuance. Again she thought of the monosyllabic utterances of those loiterers whose sole intent was to put each other down as devastatingly as possible. Then she noticed the huddled figure of Amoun on the imaginary touchline, nursing the tiny creature that had taken over his life. Titania approached him and knelt nearby. '*Selaamu aleikum*. Hello Amoun,' she said. He turned and greeted her.

'How's the baby?' she asked him.

'He's OK, but I don't think he likes the dust.'

'You could take him away from the dust,' Titania suggested, quietly.

'Where? Dust is everywhere here.' He had a point. A cheer went up: someone had scored a goal.

'Would you like me to hold little Azhar for you while you have a quick turn in the game?' Titania said, nonchalantly.

Amoun held the baby close and hesitated. 'You will stay here, won't you?' he said, suspiciously.

'Of course. I promise not to go anywhere,' Titania said reassuringly.

Eagerly, Amoun stood up. Then he paused. 'You must stay here,' he reiterated.

'I promise.' Titania took the bundle and watched the lithe boy launch himself into the game. He was only a scrap of a thing himself, but he attacked the ball like a lion.

Titania cuddled baby Azhar and listened to the excited cries of the boys. A fierce sun drained the scene of much of its colour. The odours of warm diesels, distant rubbish fires, *shisha* smoke and powdered urine filled the dusty air with that heady olfactory sensation peculiar to kamyonserais the length and breadth of the Middle East. If the baby could survive here, it would probably live for ever, she thought. Later, she went and bought some *shwerma* wraps and brought them back for the footballers. They squatted in the dust and ate cheerfully. Titania asked them for their aspirations, some of them translating for the others. Most of them wanted to stow away in lorries bound for Europe. One of them wanted to go home but couldn't pluck up the courage to go alone. Another had relatives in Damascus but didn't know how to find them.

Amoun told Titania that the boys wanted to go back to school but didn't like admitting it. 'Teach us English!' he demanded suddenly.

'Yes! Please teach us. Then we can get jobs.'

'And find things on the Internet.'

'But I'll probably be gone in a day or two's time,' Titania protested. The midday call to prayer began and the boys became dejected. A blast from Bingo's air horns caught Titania's attention, and she left a little sense of diminished hope behind in the cluster of ragged boys.

Diminished hope appeared to have stricken Bingo too. Titania found him banging about in the trailer locker with the tea things. 'Bad news?' she asked.

'Aye. The twat who owns this load has gone missing and they won't take it off, let alone clear customs for it.'

'Missing? I thought he was a teacher.'

'He is, but even the school doesn't know where he's gone, apparently.'

'Blimey.' Four Turkish artics lumbered in and created a billowing dust storm, which made Bingo even tetchier. 'We'll have to give it a day or two. Then I'll kick up. I was never happy with doing a house removal with a tilt trailer in the first place. No body would dream of such a daft idea these days. It only needs someone to slash the sides and heaven knows what would go missing.'

'I thought you said everything was nailed into shipping crates,' Titania said.

'Well yes, there is that, I suppose. Everything except the piano; that's on the arse end against the tailboard.'

'Well then, relax. Let's just have a mini-break; sit on the veranda and reconvene the Paradise Club,' Titania suggested. Bingo laughed.

'You're right. We'll bow to fate for now. Come on, let's stow all this away. I'll treat you to a kebab in the Janna.'

In the restaurant Titania drew the restaurateur, Mehmet, aside once their meal order had been placed. 'Do you order your supplies from Damascus?' she asked him.

'Some of them. Why?'

'I wondered if you could get baby milk delivered. You know – formula. Little Azhar's getting his breast milk but he just isn't being fed often enough,' Titania said.

'There's a clinic here, in the transport zone. They'll order it for you. I'll send one of those kids out there to take you round this afternoon,' Mehmet promised.

'It will need to be stored in a refrigerator. Is it possible for Amoun to keep it here, in the kitchen?'

Mehmet nodded and smiled kindly. 'Of course.'

Bingo and Titania breakfasted on the veranda again the following morning. It was raised and looked out over the compound. The sun was powerful and reflected harshly from the glasswork of moving trucks. Mehmet brought out coffee on a tray. 'One Turkish and one filter,' he said. 'Heard anything from those camel boys?'

'Not for some time,' Bingo said. 'The last email said that Ro was becoming a Muslim. They sound reasonably contented.'

'We miss them here, you know. Drivers still ask after them.'

'Well, you seem to have a new cohort to keep you busy,' Bingo laughed.

'What the Palestinian kids?' Mehmet asked, rolling his eyes. Right on cue, three of them ran past, kicking the deflated football and shouting loudly. Mehmet went indoors.

'They pleaded with me to teach them English,' Titania commented.

'These kids need tying down for some thorough basic teaching and some order in their lives,' Bingo commented.

'They need releasing, not tying down,' Titania said. 'They need education for autonomy, for self-determination. They need someone to empower them, not crush their spirits. They need help to learn the language of self-representation. You're right of course about a bit of basic teaching: the acquisition of a few skills and some useful knowledge would contribute to the process of empowerment.'

'Perhaps we should bring some old textbooks down,' Bingo suggested.

'At first,' Titania answered, 'we would have to strive to work from the individual children, not from the body of knowledge we imagine they require.'

'How could we do that?'

'Let's observe them and try to identify tangible needs. For example, if we started with Amoun, we could teach him how to care for baby Azhar and meet his hygiene and diet needs. At the same time we could show him how to meet his own basic needs without compromising the baby's. He hasn't yet worked that out and he's letting himself go unnecessarily. Do you see? We'd have to start where the boys actually are, and not where we wish they were.'

'You're right. We have a couple of days, maybe more. I'll help in any way I can. Their freedom is my freedom.'

'What motivates you to help them, Bingo?'

'Meeting the needs of kids helps me to keep in touch with my boy-self. I recognise him in the lives of these lads. In turn, that helps me to see the child-selves in the adults I meet.'

'A bit like Mother Theresa of Calcutta perceiving Christ in all her patients?'

'Not so grand, perhaps, but yes, very much the same thing, I reckon.'

'Helping Ro and Nuri in Nuweiba has had quite an impact on you, hasn't it?'

'It has. Actually, we could do with them here in Kamyonistan to help teach some English to these boys. They all seem to speak a little.'

'Peer teaching works very well,' Titania observed.

'Still, we can't very well expect Ro and Nuri to drop everything and come here. Besides, they can't abandon their camels, and they'd need visas. So you still think the childhood self is the Holy Grail, do you?'

'The complete self is probably the Holy Grail. No self is complete without the child component.'

A battered breakdown wagon had drawn up nearby and disgorged a motley crew of Arab musicians. The van suspended from the winch behind looked as if it had been involved in an accident. From the damaged van the musicians pulled a double bass, a small drum kit, two guitars and a very old accordion. Finally, a keyboard and stand emerged. The keyboard was wrecked.

Amoun appeared. He had just been to have Azhar fed. The baby was asleep. 'OK, now it's your turn to be fed,' Titania said, firmly. She reached out, in a gesture of offer, for the child. Amoun backed away. 'If you don't have food, drink and rest the same as your baby, you won't be well enough to look after him,' Titania said pointedly.

'The baby needs me,' Amoun said sulkily.

'The baby needs you to be alert, fit and well enough to meet his little needs,' Titania insisted. 'I'll sit here with Azhar, while you pop inside with Bingo for some breakfast. You can bring it out here if you like. Go on now.'

Reluctantly, he handed Azhar over. With the hiss of air brakes, an MAN drawbar outfit pulled up and the driver got out to bang all the tyres with an old mallet handle. Azhar opened his eyes, gave the equipage a withering look, compressed his lips and returned to his slumbers.

That afternoon, Bingo and Titania gathered the Palestinian boys around in the shade of their trailer and began the process of helping them to speak English. Faintly reminiscent of a couple of elderly missionaries, they perched on Turkish folding stools, Titania in her straw hat with its cerise scarf attached and Bingo in his shirtsleeves. The boys were avid learners and grew very animated when it came to naming foods. Amoun took on the role of pupil-teacher because he already knew much more English than the others. Bingo taught them to say 'trailer', which confused them because Arabic had borrowed the word to mean 'lorry and trailer combination'. Titania soon had them shaking each other's hands and greeting each other in clear English, until they all fell into helpless laughter because Azhar made his contribution by gargling and then he spat up some of his breakfast into the *shamagh*.

The arrival of two wagons from Britain brought the afternoon's lessons to a close. First to pull alongside was Jumbo, a large and jolly driver with a pirate's beard piloting a Volvo FH16 with a garment trailer. Behind him was a surprise. At the wheel of a left-hand drive Iveco Eurostar, connected to a tilt, was the transport journalist, Eric. They all knew each other.

'Got the kettle on, mate?' Jumbo called from his window.

'Just filling her up, Jumbo. Bring your mug, will you!' Bingo yelled above the din of engines. The boys dispersed, except for Amoun who remained.

'So what are you doing driving a wagon?' Bingo demanded of Eric.

'I don't know. Sudden rush of shit to the brain, I think. I had a bit of a cash flow crisis because the magazine wanted to shelve several articles until autumn. Then this job came up,' Eric said.

'Permanent, is it?'

'Oh no! This wagon's a seller. I'm tipping in Saudi, running empty into Qatar and flogging it in Doha.'

'Then flying home to write more articles?'

'More or less. Might do another seller if there's one going.' Eric shrugged.

'Are you making tea or ain't you?' Jumbo demanded. 'My stomach thinks my throat's been slit.'

'Nearly there, mate. Are you going to Saudi too?'

'Nope,' Jumbo said sitting back in his garden chair and beaming.

'Well, is it a secret then?' Bingo demanded. 'Will you have to kill me if you tell me?'

'Here!' Jumbo announced, triumphantly. 'I'm tipping and loading here.'

'Blimey!' Bingo said. 'You might have to drink beer tonight then!'

'Of course! It'd be bloody rude not to,' Jumbo replied. Eric reached for his sun hat behind the driver's seat and a plastic water bottle containing yellow liquid fell to the ground. Jumbo laughed and said, 'You take my advice, Eric. Keep your piss bottle in a separate place, away from your drinking water. I was driving from Dresden to Rostock one morning after I'd been on the beer the night before, when I took two big swigs from my water bottle. I knew by the taste it wasn't the right one.'

'You're an animal, Jumbo,' Eric laughed.

'Well, it's all right if it's fresh. Won't do you no harm. It tasted exactly like that alcohol-free lager. That's probably how they make it: drink beer, piss it and bottle it. I wouldn't mind that job.'

'The amount you put away, mate, you could do it the other way round: drink alcohol-free lager, piss beer and bottle it. Wouldn't even have to tell customs and excise,' Eric said.

'All this talk of beer, and we haven't got a drop on the table!' Bingo put in.

'Come on then,' Eric said. 'The sun's nearly over the mirror arm. Let's adjourn to the Plot-Loss Arms and encourage Mehmet to indulge us with intoxicating liquids.'

'He's been like this all the way down, you know. We'll make a driver of him yet!' Jumbo chuckled.

'Cheeky monkey!' Eric retorted. They stowed the gear, locked up and headed for the Janna.

'Where's Amoun? I didn't see him go,' Titania said.

'He's gone to diesel up his nipper,' Jumbo answered.

'With any luck, his baby milk should arrive tomorrow. I couldn't have made it plainer to the man in the clinic!' Titania sighed.

Kamyonistan Café Band

The sight of three British drivers creating a classic fry-up in their shorts and vests had long been accepted as an institution in the Middle East at breakfast time. Now that such creatures were such a rarity, however, it had become something of a spectator sport. Among those coaxed from the fabric of Kamyonistan by the smell of cooking bacon were two Palestinian boys and the van-load of Arab musicians. Titania saw to the tea while the drivers, for all the world as if they were at a village barbecue, ensured that breakfast was fried to perfection. Cardboard boxes had been unflattened to provide screens around the gas burners to prevent the wind from disturbing the flames.

Bacon being *haram*, the musicians were content to drink tea and watch Kamyonistan's answer to *Wildlife on One*. Ensconced in garden chairs, performers in the cultural demonstration did not disappoint: eating pig meat using the left hand was the star attraction, while the appearance of two bottles of red wine to wash down breakfast brought gasps of amazement. Showing great sensitivity, the musicians refrained from applause, but when the following act commenced, they rose to their feet and clapped enthusiastically. A boy carrying a brown *shamagh* emerged from stage left, just as the lady in the straw hat was disinfecting a washing-up bowl and refilling it with tepid water. The young boy then delighted his audience by producing a newborn infant from the *shamagh* and bathing the tiny thing with utmost tenderness under the guidance of the English lady. It was better than telly, they told each other.

The third act comprised a trio of customs officers who entered from stage right and moved the focal point to the rear of Bingo's trailer. Here, they supervised while Bingo broke the seal and presented it, opened the back of the tilt, lowered the tailboard and pushed the rear flap of the canopy onto the roof of the trailer.

Once again, the musicians rose to their feet, but this time in awed silence; for there, on the tailboard, was an upright piano. All eyes were on the customs officers, who climbed among the shipping crates, prising some open, while Bingo nailed them back down behind them, so nobody noticed that the musicians had slipped away. Checklists were scrutinised and ticked. The freight agent appeared and then left with the customs men.

'Can I close up the back?' Bingo asked.

'No, we're returning,' the agent announced.

When Bingo turned to tell Titania what was happening, the musicians were standing there, complete with guitar, violin, double bass, drums and accordion. It was too good an opportunity to miss. There was sufficient space on the tailboard to rotate the piano and draw up a packing case for a stool. Suddenly, the audience had become the performers and there was music. It was fantastic music; vibrant, lively stuff that evoked the streets of Cairo, the piazzas of Rome and the bars of Romania all at the same time. There were strains of café arabesque and the plaintive calls of Anatolian shepherds. Then the accordion wheezed and died. Along with the keyboard, it had been damaged in the accident and now it had stopped functioning completely. Bingo ran to Amoun and shouted instructions at him. Then he pleaded with him, and finally Amoun handed Azhar to Titania and ran off at speed.

Tea and wine were consumed in equal measure. Syrian and Turkish drivers drifted across the compound to see what was happening. Amoun returned with Mahmout, the youth from the truck wash. He was carrying an accordion, once played by a boy named Tariq who was gifted, but who had died in a suicide attack. This accordion had preyed on Bingo's mind, and now at last it would see service. Delighted, the accordionist tried it out before pronouncing it better than his own. The band played a short piece, at the end of which Mahmout presented the instrument to the accordionist and embraced him. During the next piece, which resembled oriental swing, Bingo's freight agent returned, alone. He informed Bingo that the owner of the goods was in prison and that the load would be taken off and put into storage, but he didn't know when.

Inevitably, before the load was re-secured that morning, the piano was spirited into Restaurant Janna by simply reversing the trailer onto the veranda and lifting it off: naughty, but fun.

'We'll have a bit of a knees-up tonight, lads!' Jumbo chuckled. Mehmet interviewed the musicians at length; then he announced that the band was from Damascus and that they had been booked to perform in Aleppo that evening, so they were happy to perform their programme for the weary truckers of the TIR trail instead. Jumbo was given permission to tip, so he spent the rest of the afternoon backed onto a loading bay in a neighbouring warehouse.

Titania's afternoon was spent shopping. She entered a jungle of thick shadows in the drivers' souk, where awnings were strung from the shops to the hulks of derelict trailers. Sun-dappled trestles stood laden with lorry parts, local produce and faded tourist tat from Damascus. Titania wished that she had brought a boy to haggle on her behalf. Then she spotted the very item she had come for: a burner for their gas bottle. Bingo's had been sheared near the base, when a box of groceries had dropped onto it while the lorry was being manoeuvred onto the veranda that morning. Probably divine providence, she thought super-stitiously. Titania bought it, wondering at this strange breed of drivers who used high-tech vehicles but who were content to utilise primitive burners without regulators or reliable valves. They were latter-day trappers and merchant adventurers at heart, she decided. 'A lot of the drivers who used to come down here were social misfits,' Jumbo had told her. 'Don't get me wrong, some of the best blokes I've ever met have come down on the Middle East run, and they were true gentlemen of the road. But among them were some really nasty, bullying criminal types who would think nothing of cheating a fellow driver. They could be your best friend or your worst enemy.'

An old Turkish driver summed up the lasting impression these rogues had left behind them on the TIR trail when Titania had asked him what he feared most on the Middle East run. 'British drivers,' he had answered, without hesitation. 'They're a liability! They get drunk at every opportunity and want to fight everybody. Then they squander or lose their running money and expect everyone else to provide for them. I'm glad to see the back of them down here. I used to avoid parking anywhere near them – except for Jumbo here, of course – but he used to come in the "Turk-parks" with us, didn't you, Jumbo!'

Pushing past a produce-laden donkey, Titania noticed clusters of hanging, Arab-pattern *shamaghs*, one of which was brown. Music boomed out of a nearby doorway. She asked for the brown *shamagh*; it would make a nice little gift for Amoun. Titania sailed into her own state of paradise: shopping.

That evening, the atmosphere in the Janna was very lively. Word had got round and drivers from all over the Middle East were eating, sipping *shay*, smoking *shisha* or simple chatting. The usual noisy Arabic pop music was absent and the band was warming up. Titania persuaded Amoun to take Azhar onto the veranda to keep him out of the smoky atmosphere, not to mention the noise. Amoun had now discovered the joys of bottle-feeding his little treasure, and as the novelty of this had yet to wear off, he was reluctant to yield Azhar to Titania's care.

Bingo, Titania, Eric and Jumbo were sitting at a table well stocked with cans of beer. Eric was saying, 'I learned to double-declutch on a piano. It had pedals and a music stand upon which to prop an old AA driving manual.'

'What did you use for a gearstick then, mate?' Jumbo asked.

'It only had two pedals. I think it must have been an automatic!' Eric replied. They laughed. The music started. It was like a switch being thrown, for the room filled instantly with magic. Titania was transported. She smiled dreamily to herself. Someone touched her shoulder and she turned. Amoun stepped aside and there, next to him, stood two smiling boys: Ro and Nuri.

After a good deal of hugging, Ro introduced Wahid to Bingo who pressed a beer into the Jordanian driver's hand and gave him his chair. Bingo berated Ro good-naturedly for quitting Egypt without first forming a plan, but in reality he was relieved to see him. Ro protested that coming to Kamyonistan was a plan in its own right and that giving plans time to incubate was not necessarily a virtue, particularly with the hot breath of the police on one's neck. Bingo conceded. Ro declined an offer of beer. Refusing circumcision was one thing; drinking alcohol was quite another, he thought, looking at the beer-swilling fellow Muslim driver, for whom the reverse was evidently true.

Drawn into the bewitching sound of the music, Ro and Nuri relaxed and ceased to fret, temporarily, about their lost camels. The band was playing a number made famous by the Lebanese singer, Fayrouz. Jumbo, returning from a trip to the hole in the floor, broke into a surprisingly graceful imitation of the sand dance and brought the house down. 'That man's got an accordion just like Tariq used to have!' Ro shouted to Bingo above the laughter. Bingo just gave him the thumbs up and grinned.

Mahmout, the contents of whose jeans, on a previous trip, Bingo had been made familiar with, passed in front of their table and gave Bingo the glad eye. Bingo rose as one hypnotised. Titania said, 'Where do you think you're going?'

Bingo leaned over to her and replied, 'With respect to Elroy Flecker, my dear...

> "I travel not for trafficking alone,
> By hot exhausts I make my cunning plan;
> To seek to blow what should not be blown,
> I take the gold road to Kamyonistan." '

'Well, just you be careful!' Titania laughed.

'Don't worry, I won't spill a drop.'

With those words, he followed the youth into the night.

Amoun was feeding Azhar on the veranda when Nuri and Ro joined him. There ensued lively talk among them, for much had happened in the eighteen or so months since they had last met. So it came to pass that a baby travelling from birth to babyhood fell among boys who doted on him, marvelled at the engaging, nuzzling creature and took him into their hearts. 'Is our lorry still there?' Ro asked. 'You know, the one we lived in.'

'No. They took the tractor unit away ages ago. I think it's in the scrapyard next to the workshops. The trailer stayed there for a long time, but I think that's gone too,' Amoun told them.

It would be strange to see Kamyonistan in the daylight again, Ro thought. Amoun said as an afterthought, 'Your *shamagh* stayed tied to the mirror for months, until the wind blew it ragged.' Ro glanced at Nuri and felt unsettling memories flooding back. He wondered whether they had been wise to return.

Amoun handed the baby to Ro saying, 'Hold him for a minute will you, I must do a wee!' Then Jumbo wobbled out, gave the little bundle a prod and said, 'Reckon he could do with an oil change, don't you?' Someone began to sing with the musicians.

Nuri turned to Ro. 'Where are we going to sleep tonight?' Ro hadn't given it a thought.

'Under Jumbo's trailer, I suppose.'

Destination Kamyonistan

Surprisingly, the next day began cool and misty. Cloud rolled down the mountain and swirled eerily about the truck stop. Woken early by the chill, Ro and Nuri wandered down the narrow aisles created by standing lorries until the corner minaret loomed out of the gloom. A muffled cockcrow was the only sound. They could almost have been in the back streets of Cairo or Istanbul. Nuri paused in front of a Scania 143 Topline with a Bulgarian tilt trailer. 'Let's try the minaret,' he said, mischievously.

The boys went to the foot of the minaret and heaved on the door. It was locked. 'I bet that's been shut since we locked it,' Ro said. 'What did we do with the key?'

'We used to have a secret place for things like that, do you remember? In the ERF.'

'Oh yes,' Ro said. 'Under the lining in one of the cupboards. Let's see if we can find the ERF later.'

By mid-morning, sunlight was dripping from the palm fronds and the mist had been burnt off, leaving behind the thinnest of vapours. Titania sat with Ro and Nuri in front of Bingo's wagon.

'Isn't it idyllic!' Eric shouted above his engine, which was roaring away on fast tick over.

'I don't know about that,' Ro muttered gloomily. 'We need to get work and we haven't got camels, brushes or anything.'

'Well I can give you a temporary job in return for food and basic upkeep until Bingo gets unloaded and reloaded,' Titania announced, brightly.

'What do you mean?' Ro asked.

Titania told the two boys about her ad hoc English lessons for the Palestinians. 'While I think about it,' she said later, 'the solicitor who dealt with your uncle Norman's estate when he was killed, traced your name to my address. You were right in thinking that he had little to leave, but you have either under-estimated or overlooked the extent of your inheritance following the death of your mother. Legally, you have no access to it until you are eighteen. I have all the paperwork at home. I'll get a copy of everything sent to you here if you are staying here. Also, I can't remember if we told you at the time; Bingo and I took out full travel and health insurance for both of you when you stayed behind in Egypt. We felt uncomfortable about letting you survive there on your own, so we took the precaution. I'll get that paperwork to you as well.'

'Thanks,' Ro said. 'Eighteen seems a bit late. We need it now!'

'Yes, well, your mother would have assumed you were at school till eighteen, not gallivanting round the Middle East like a nomad!' Titania replied.

Amoun was the first to arrive, followed by Hamid and the others. From the outset, a jolly atmosphere prevailed. Greetings merged into the verbal labelling of food, which in turn degener-ated into the naming of body parts and inevitable hilarity. Eric brought them fresh mango juice at half-time. Deprivation had not diminished their appetite for useful knowledge and education began to take place at all sorts of levels in an organic way. In addition to language acquisition, topics of interest ranged, that morning, from the care of trailer tyres to the best techniques for bathing baby Azhar. The honing of interpersonal skills formed part of the hidden curriculum, and in no time at all Titania found herself at the close of a teaching session in which learning had taken place without recourse to elaborate, prescriptive plans. Football rounded off the morning, and bean soup was taken on the veranda, where Wahid joined them while he waited to unload.

In the drowsy heat of afternoon, a tired looking trailer loafed in the dust nearby, while listless breezes caught its curtain straps and let them clang against the raves. Its load was being tran-shipped onto a scruffy, short-pin, twelve-metre, step-frame tilt drawn by a flat roofed, unmarked Volvo F10. A skylark sang above the arid landscape. Cab curtains were half-drawn against the glare and the faint smell of distant hay hung among the wagons.

Ro and Nuri crept off, eager to find the ERF. In the scrapyard, they had trouble convincing the guardian that they were not there to steal parts. Reluctantly, he took them to a bank of wrecked vehicles. The ERF had been extensively cannibalised, and at first it did not look as if the boys would be able to get at it, let alone into it. In the end Ro had to climb through the passenger window. It was too dirty and chaotic in the cab to explore memories. He made straight for the hiding place. Sure enough, there was the key to the minaret. There was an envelope too. He took it out and examined it. It meant nothing to him, but he pocketed it. Down the side of the driver's seat he found a copy of the magazine with Eric's article about the camel wash inside. Also, he found the translations of prayers that Mehmet had given him all that time ago. Suddenly, he realised that it was too hot in the cab and he crawled out.

Making sure that no one had seen them, Ro and Nuri made their way to the minaret in the corner where their truck had once stood. They turned the key and scrambled up the narrow, tight staircase until they emerged onto the little balcony, high above the TIR-parking compound. 'There's Bingo's wagon,' Ro said, pointing.

'And there's Amoun feeding his baby,' Nuri said. He looked down at all the miniature lorries scattered across the great compound. What if boys could fly? he thought. Ro's mind snatched at a vague memory of Nuri suggesting that boys might fly. They were no longer boys in the sense that they were then, he reflected a little sadly. A good deal of unhappy water had flowed under the bridge since their carefree days in Kamyonistan. The two world-weary teenagers stood silently for a moment. Then Ro remembered the envelope. He pulled it out and opened it. In it was the receipt for the cash he'd changed on Christmas Day when Nuri had been ill. The other item was a small coin. He looked at it. Nuri took it from him and began to giggle delightedly. 'Iraq!' Nuri said, enigmatically.

'Iraq?'

'Yes. This is the coin pillaged from the Baghdad museum after the invasion. Don't you remember? A driver had it in the restaurant and I swallowed it. He was really angry. We had to buy him lunch.'

Ro did remember and soon he too was laughing. Then Nuri

pointed into the compound that lay beyond the diesel pumps. 'Look at all those army trucks! It's like that time we thought Damascus was going to be air raided.' There were tanks too and heavy artillery.

'Come on,' Ro said. 'We don't want to be seen up here with all that military hardware floating about!' They descended and locked the door.

They found Eric standing in the middle of the TIR parking, shading his eyes against the sun. 'Look at this lot!' Eric said. No truck ever failed to interest Eric. He was watching a convoy of a dozen or so artics crawl across the compound in a huge cloud of dust. 'Iranians,' Eric said.

Ro couldn't see the details on the number plates. 'How can you tell?' he asked.

'Those oversize tyres, for one thing,' Eric answered. 'Then there are the trailers: all Iranian-built tilts; you can tell by the style. Plus, all the tractor units are six-by-four Iveco Eurotrakkers, which are quite popular with the Iranians. Good on the desert roads.'

'They've got a police escort,' observed Ro.

'No,' Eric corrected. 'It's a military one.'

'I wonder what they're carrying,' Nuri said.

'Probably best not to enquire too closely,' Eric advised. 'The Iranians are very pally with Syria at the moment, and the Americans and Israelis are none too happy about it.'

The lorries looked very imposing, standing as they did so high off the ground. Both the Eurotrakkers and the Iran-spec tilts boasted good ground clearance quite apart from the fact that they ran on big tyres. When they had run their truck-wash business here using camels, Nuri and Ro had always liked the Iranian drivers. For one thing, they nearly always spoke good English; and for another, they were always friendly.

The trio ambled back to the veranda where the sun had evidently set over the mirror-arm. Amoun was coping with baby Azhar who, in an industrious mood, was busy firing at both ends. Effortlessly, Amoun mopped up while he helped Hamid to pronounce English words of greeting and welcome.

Jumbo looked up and said to Eric, 'Hello, mate! We were

wondering just now what transmission you've got in that Eurostar of yours. I know you've got a 520 lump in it because I tried to leave you behind coming up Bolu!'

'It did have a SAMT semi-automated transmission in it, but apparently it was converted. It now has a manual Twin Splitter: proper gearbox, mate.'

'Don't start Eric on lorry gearboxes, for crying out loud!' Bingo put in. 'Give him beer, quick, to make him forget them. Anyway, when are you going to Doha?'

At that moment the band struck up behind them in the restaurant. Eric laughed. 'Ah! The Kamyonistan Café Band! I'm in no hurry,' he said, taking a bottle from Jumbo.

'At least it's nice and sunny here,' Jumbo commented. 'It was a bit chilly coming up Bolu; I had to put the fire on for an hour or so.'

Titania appeared and said, 'Bingo, I wonder if that bloke has any language teaching materials in that load of yours.'

'We can't go rummaging through someone else's possessions!' Bingo protested.

'No, but customs can.'

'Forget it,' Bingo said. 'If that was your stuff, you'd expect me to protect it from marauding *gumruk* officials and dotty schoolteachers.'

'*Gumruk*?'

'Customs.'

'What about the piano, then?'

'That was different. We didn't have to rummage and it's easily put back.'

'You either misappropriated it or you didn't!'

'Think grey. Don't think black and white.'

'Oi! Have a beer, you two, and stop bickering like an old couple. Get that music, man!'

Across the TIR parking, the Iranian trucks were on the move again, kicking up dust as they were escorted into a neighbouring compound. Eric chatted to the drivers about them. Then Jumbo asked if anyone had heard the news recently. Bingo said, 'I like to keep abreast of the news if I possibly can – especially down here.'

'So do I,' Eric said. 'I have noticed that quite a lot of military traffic comes in here.'

'When we were living here,' Ro said, 'loads of military containers used to come in. Ordinary civilian lorries carried them,
but there were army lorries as well.'

'Do you remember the blackouts we had, when the boy
soldiers thought the Americans or the Israelis were going to bomb
Damascus with aircraft?' Nuri said.

'You never told us about that, Ro!' Bingo said. He looked
concerned.

'I'd forgotten till today,' Ro replied.

'We really thought we might die, didn't we, Ro,' Nuri
prompted. Ro remembered.

Mehmet arrived to wipe the tables. 'I've been talking to the
receptionist in an orphanage,' he said, chattily.

'About Azhar?' Titania asked.

'They say they haven't room for babies and that they're send-
ing a kid up here they can't cope with,' Mehmet said. 'I'll be
honest; as soon as I mentioned refugees, she lost interest.'

'Great,' Titania said, ironically.

'Flies!' Jumbo muttered, flapping at his forehead. 'That's what
gets me in the desert. You can be in the middle of nowhere in
Saudi, having a roadside brew, when suddenly 20,000 flies turn
up. Where the hell do they come from?'

Bingo ambled to the edge of the veranda. His sundowners had
gone to his head rather and he was briefly overcome with
euphoria. Inexplicably, the old hymn, 'For the Beauty of the
Earth', entered his mind. He was transported to a drowsy
summer's day when, aged about ten, he'd stood in the middle of a
field full of butterflies and sung the hymn, which he'd learnt at
school. The sensation of at-oneness-with-the-world was identical;
except, he remembered, at ten he hadn't required sundowners to
achieve it. Bingo sighed and reflected that children didn't need
alcohol because they were still there, in paradise. He felt protective towards this precious child within, but the moment itself was
in no need of protection, for it was unassailable in the first place.
In a sense, he decided, this was original joy he was feeling just as
he had experienced original pain when he had compared his rite
of passage with Ro's that time. The trick was to recognise that this
moment too, over fifty years later, was unassailable and that it

was, furthermore, attainable without alcohol. Pausing, glass in hand, he watched Ro and Nuri walking in front of an approaching Kenworth K100E Aerodyne in impressive condition. Bingo turned to call Eric. He wouldn't rob Eric of this happy indulgence in sunset truck watching.

Ro and Nuri had slipped away to the drivers' mosque. The imam spoke no English and understood little of Ro's quirky Arabic. He remembered them from their previous sojourn, however, and he welcomed them with open arms. When Nuri told him that Ro had come to pray, he was delighted. They knew that he had been fully aware of their controversial relationship but he made no attempt to judge or condemn. Perhaps, thought Nuri, he was of Mehmet's school of thinking.

Kamyonistan Beleaguered

Hamid, the bigger Palestinian boy, was repairing an old camping table for Eric. Eric was packing his locker and announcing his intention to leave in the afternoon. Titania was teaching English words to a huddle of boys. Amoun, Ro and Nuri were bathing Azhar in the shade of the trailer. The arrival of a police car unsettled the boys. It pulled up on the shady side of the F10 that they had seen loading the previous day. Two officers climbed out and propelled a smaller figure before them. The kid was wearing a denim jacket and nondescript trousers. At first, Ro thought that the step-frame tilt was the object of their attention, but the three figures made their way towards the boys.

'It's Salah!' Hamid muttered in horror. The boys crowded round. Then they shook hands with her and some of them hugged her uncertainly. Ro was unable to follow their Arabic, but Nuri gave him the gist.

'What happened? Why aren't you dead?' Hamid asked.

'I woke up in hospital. I'm all right now, just a bit weak and sore,' came the reply.

'But Salah – we can't call you that now you're a girl. What shall we call you?'

'Aysha. My real name's Aysha,' she said. 'Is this my baby?' Amoun looked alarmed.

'Yes,' Hamid said. 'Here, hold him.' He prised the infant from Amoun's grasp. Satisfied that all was well, the policemen announced that they would be back for Aysha and her baby when there was room for them in the orphanage. They left, looking relieved.

Aysha looked at the strange little thing cradled in the denim crook of her arm. She did not know what to say. Ro volunteered, 'He's the sweetest baby who ever graced the earth!'

'He owes his life to Amoun,' Nuri said. 'He's cared for him

night and day. You should be grateful to him.' They turned to Amoun. He had vanished.

'He's called Azhar,' one boy added.

'He came with a name?' Aysha asked, confused. She recovered her wits. 'So you named him, then?'

'Amoun did. He's been his mum – and his dad,' Hamid said. 'Where is he?'

A few minutes later, they found Amoun behind the F10 and step-frame tilt. He sat, bereft, with his head in his arms, weeping silently, devoid of any sense of purpose. Titania perceived in an instant that this was going to be a problem. Her schoolteacher's instincts told her to intervene immediately and suggest that a handover period should be negotiated, and that thereafter Amoun and Aysha might share the parenting for a while. However, Titania's deeper instincts told her to step back and observe, allowing a natural solution to evolve. In the event, Azhar made the decision for them by howling inconsolably. Flustered, Aysha looked round for support. For a brief moment, her eyes appealed to the only other woman present. Titania simply nodded in Amoun's direction and Aysha took the hint. She approached the sobbing boy and stood in front of him. Amoun stood up and Aysha pushed the baby into his familiar arms. Tenderly, Amoun brushed the baby's cheek with his lips and both children stopped crying. He pulled a half-finished bottle of milk from his pocket, cleaned the teet by sucking it and popped it into the tiny mouth.

'It can have a mum and a dad too, now,' Nuri said happily. 'Why don't you share him for a little while?'

'I rest my case,' Titania said to herself, smiling. She was rather looking forward to the prospect of Aysha being shown how to bath her baby by the little lad.

By way of consolation, Ro and Nuri decided to show Amoun their minaret. After all, they had used it to spy on him all that time ago. Delighted, he handed the sleeping Azhar to his mother and raced off with them among the parked lorries. They puffed and panted up the stifling staircase and climbed onto the balcony to view Kamyonistan.

'Wow! Where did all those army trucks come from?' Amoun asked, when he raised his eyes to the neighbouring compounds.

'That unfinished warehouse over there,' Ro said. 'Isn't that where you lot used to live before the army cleared it? You know, with Tariq and Ahmad?'

'Yes. I haven't been there since. It gives me the creeps,' Amoun said.

'Look down there, next to the warehouse,' Ro said. 'That's where all those Iranian trucks have gone.'

It came out of the ether. Transfixed, the boys watched it catch the afternoon sunlight as it raced in their direction. The rocket hit the warehouse with a terrific shudder. Instinctively, the boys ducked. The minaret shook alarmingly. Everything beyond the truck-stop vanished in a wall of dust. A second blast came from slightly further away. Finally, another came from behind them.

'Azhar!' Amoun cried, and ran for the stairs.

'Wait!' Ro shouted.

'Come on, Ro, it's dangerous up here!' Nuri yelled, pulling at his friend.

'Hang on, just for a minute. Let's see what's been hit.' He leaned over the rail.

Nuri loitered, restlessly. 'You won't see anything with all that dust,' he protested.

'We should be above the worst of it here. Look, the rocket missed nearly all these army trucks.' They watched as dozens of men ran about trying to make sense of the attack. 'I don't think anything's fallen into the actual truck stop,' Ro continued. 'It's difficult to see with all this dust.'

'And smoke!' Nuri added. Flames were roaring from the warehouse. A series of explosions erupted from the site and smoke obliterated everything. Ro turned to the door.

Down in the TIR compound, the air was foul with smoke and dust. Covering their mouths they picked their way among the wagons. Poor visibility impaired their sense of direction. Ahead of them they could see two or three lorries pushed over, partly on their sides, leaning at odd angles into one another. The wall was breached at this point and the stone blocks had jammed against them. The boys checked to see if any drivers were injured, but the location was deserted. 'We're going in the wrong direction,' Ro said. 'This is the other end of our old wall.'

Heading into the middle of the compound, they took their luck. It was impossible to navigate by parked lorries. Somewhere, a siren was wailing. Then, very close, they heard the muezzin's call to prayer. 'We must be at the drivers' mosque!' Nuri said.

'Let's see if our secret garden's still there!' Ro said.

'Are you mad? We're under attack. What about the others?'

'They'll be all right,' Ro said, serenely. 'You saw that no rockets went inside the truck-stop part.' Following their ears, Ro and Nuri entered the precincts, and in the grey-brown light they found themselves in the garden. Standing under the dust-coated lemon trees and facing the bank of suspended bougainvillea, it felt doubly surreal for being at once somewhere that held special memories for them and at the same time being a weird place to stand during an assault.

'It's a funny sort of paradise garden today,' Ro remarked.

'It's still a paradise garden, though, isn't it?'

'The prophet Isa – Jesus – said that it's easier for a camel to pass through the eye of a needle than it is for a rich man to enter the gates of paradise.'

'You'd never get the camel to stand still long enough,' Nuri said.

'You'd have to liquidise it first, then inject the fluid through the eye of the needle with a hypodermic syringe,' Ro said authoritatively.

Nuri giggled and briefly, they hugged each other. 'Come on, let's go. *Yallah!*'

Bingo's wagon stood silently in the murky light. There was no sign of life in Eric's or Jumbo's either. 'They'll be in the Janna. Come on,' Ro urged.

The atmosphere in the Janna was charged with a sense of crisis. Mehmet looked scared. Groups of drivers stood with fragments of cloth over their mouths. Jumbo turned and greeted them. Eric said, 'Quick, wet your *shamaghs* and hold them over your mouths. That could well have been an arsenal of chemical weapons that blew up.'

'It didn't blow up,' Ro said. 'We've been attacked by three rockets. We saw them from up the minaret.' Jumbo wanted to hear about it.

'Where are Bingo and Titania?' Ro asked.

'Gone to look for you.'

'Have you seen Amoun?'

'We thought he was with you.'

'Let's go and find them,' Ro suggested.

'Better to stay here and let them find you,' Jumbo said. Outside, they could hear pandemonium. Mehmet fussed and clucked. 'We're lucky to have any electricity,' he said.

Bingo and Titania arrived. 'The Turks are standing by their wagons. They fear looters,' Bingo announced.

'What's the point of that?' Eric asked. 'If they're going to loot, they'll do it whether we're standing on duty or not!'

'Hear, hear!' Jumbo boomed. 'Much wiser to stand in here and guard the beer. Talking of which, who's ready for a quick restorative?'

'What's this, the Dunkirk spirit?' Bingo enquired. 'Mine's a pint.'

Amoun turned up with Aysha in tow. She was holding Azhar a little awkwardly. 'He's very trusting,' Amoun told her. 'But you have to trust him too.'

Five minutes later, all the members of the Kamyonistan Café Band, as Jumbo liked to call them, arrived escorting the rest of the Palestinian boys. Amoun told Nuri that the musicians had gone to look for them and had brought them in as guests.

'What are you doing with wet cloths over your mouths?' Bingo laughed. Eric told him.

'Blimey!' Bingo retorted. 'You'll be suggesting we paint the inside of our windscreens white, in case of nuclear fallout next!'

Jumbo bought the musicians drinks and was merrily chatting away with the double-bass player, when the lights went out. In the twilight, life continued until Mehmet brought candles out. Shortly afterwards, Mahmout appeared with a clutch of hurricane lamps. 'But there's no paraffin,' Mehmet protested.

'No problem, we'll fill them with diesel,' Eric suggested. He turned to Ro and Nuri. 'Come on,' he said.

The air outside was unpleasantly acrid. Sure enough, many drivers were patrolling near their trucks for fear of looters. Eric unlocked his filler cap and went to his side locker, from which he retrieved a length of hose. While the boys undid all the caps on the lanterns, Eric sucked at the hose. 'When we had belly tanks under the trailer,' he said, 'this sort of thing was easier. All we had to do was to attach a fixed hose to the red air line, turn on the tap and blow as much diesel out of the belly tank as we wanted. Now, we can't have taps; we can't have belly tanks; we can't take loads of nice, cheap diesel out of the country any more. All the fun's gone out of this work.'

'There's more than enough excitement in it for me,' Ro commented dryly. They carried the dripping lamps back to the restaurant.

'We ought to get ourselves out of here, really,' Bingo was saying. 'If this place is a target, then we don't want to be here.' A uniformed man pushed his way past. Bingo stopped him. 'Is it possible to drive out of here, chief?' he asked.

The man looked puzzled. Nuri came to his rescue. The man shook his head and gestured a bit. Nuri turned to Bingo. 'He says that the gate has been damaged, and that in any case, one of the rockets destroyed the service road.'

'That must have been the one that fell behind us,' Ro said.

The piano sounded and the violin joined in. Someone applauded. Jumbo was regaling Titania with a cautionary tale. 'I had five hours left on the tacho to reach Antwerp and I was straight on the bay and loaded by half past four. By half six I was dieseling up and that's when I looked at the paperwork again...' The accordionist took up the melody and ran with it. 'But I hadn't put my watch on, 'cos I always used to leave it on English time on European work...' Deftly, the percussionist insinuated himself into the song. 'I knew that if I gave it some licks up to the border I'd make it before the tax ran out and probably make the two o'clock ferry and all...' Guitar chords rang out and a singer took up the chorus. 'They told me I'd better deliver it on effing time or else! I wasn't going to be swore at down the phone! I don't swear at them!' Jumbo paused for effect.

'Go on, Jumbo. What did you say?' Eric asked, having started to listen to the story.

'I told him, any more phone calls like that and I'd tear his bloody head off and shit down his neck.' Eric laughed. For a delicious moment, Titania stayed the censoring hand of political correctness to admire the sheer style, the panache, the imagery and the outrageous hyperbole. What a handy little put-down it would have made in the weekly staff meeting at her school. Never mind your scathing, 'Don't swear at me, Mrs Smith, please; rudeness is never necessary.' Skip the preliminary shots across the bows, reach for the smelling salts and go straight for the biggie. She glanced across at Amoun and Aysha who were sitting head-to-head, meeting the baby's needs together and each other's in doing so.

'Finger-written in the grime on the back of his trailer,' Bingo was telling Eric and Jumbo, 'was the message, "A dog is not for Christmas, it's for life." Underneath that, someone else had put, "A turkey is not for life, it's for Christmas." ' They laughed. Soup appeared, with lashings of bread.

'Mehmet!' Jumbo shouted. 'Does anyone know who's lobbing rockets at us yet?'

Mehmet looked harassed and shook his head. 'This is a military target, I'm afraid,' he said. The band played into the evening.

Being young and foolish, Ro and Nuri slipped out and walked across the compound under bright stars. They climbed their minaret and onto the balcony. Fires were burning fiercely in the military compounds, but when they moved round the balcony and stood, hand in hand, facing the mountains, they could see Syria before them washed with silver moonlight. 'We should build a house here,' Nuri said, 'on the site where the ERF stood.'

'Then we'd have our very own minaret again.'

'It's funny to think that it may still be here 1,000 years after we've gone,' Nuri said.

'Where would we put the camels?' Ro asked. He rested his head against Nuri's and let the starlight into his eyes. Their world was changing quickly, but for a moment it stopped still.

Diesel Gypsies

At sunrise, thick powdery dust laced with ash and soot coated everything. Windscreens were opaque. Debris jettisoned by explosions was strewn across the compound. Throughout the night the fire fighters and engineers could be heard working under floodlights with their own generators. The sirens of ambulances and police cars had howled relentlessly. Now, the thump of generators could still be heard. Somewhere in the direction of the road, a heavy bulldozer was labouring.

Bingo fired up the engine to let it run on fast tickover. He thought of the start of his journey, which had taken him across the luxuriant Garden of England, where shimmering sheets of deep violet bluebells had lain in woodlands bordered with lacy Umbelliferae. Titania's mind, too, had wandered as far as possible from the uncomfortable sense of being under siege. She thought of her school choir performing Elgar's enchanting choral setting, 'The Snow'. They had sung it in three-part harmony at the leavers' service. How those girls had thrown themselves into rehearsing it, always demanding to do the scrummy middle section, with its suspended harmonies, once more with feeling… A hot breeze blew into the cab. Bingo was barking into his mobile phone outside.

Titania arose and stood in the sunshine. 'Any news?'

'All I can find out is that apparently Syria has complained that Israel has fired at what it thinks is a potential threat to its security. This happened a year or two back in the north of Syria. You may remember it,' Bingo said.

'Someone's probably watching us via a satellite at this very moment. Nothing's private any more,' Titania grumbled.

'I know. Just when you think you've escaped from the invasive cameras of Blighty, you find yourself on some American spy satellite. Well, we won't get much work done today!' A man in a baseball cap was walking towards them: the freight agent. He ducked under a line of now filthy washing that was strung between Eric's and Jumbo's trucks.

'Well, well! What brings you here? First tell us about the attack,' Bingo demanded.

'I know nothing. Probably Israel.'

'Doesn't your TV news say anything?'

'No. I doubt if we'll hear more than a bulletin mentioning that a rocket fell somewhere in Syria,' the agent said. 'You can unload today. The gate is damaged, but if you drive slowly and turn right, not left, you can get out. You need to go to the Kamyonistan-TIR compound and report to warehouse twelve. They'll take it off for you there. They were originally going to deliver it in Damascus in any case.' He checked the seal on the back and departed.

'Nothing robs a man of his dignity more than a baseball cap,' Bingo observed. He climbed up and cleaned the windscreen. 'I'll get my arse round there now to show willing. They might even take it off before lunch.'

Twenty minutes later Bingo's lorry was slowly making its way across the rough ground towards the main gate. Titania went to the wash block. On the way she met Hamid and greeted him. 'Why do they do this thing to us?' Hamid demanded, gesturing at the debris.

'Because they're scared,' Titania answered. 'Why else would they do it?'

Hamid pointed to two distant figures huddled together on the veranda. 'They are lovers, I think!' He shook his head sadly. She looked across, expecting to see Ro and Nuri, but instead she saw Amoun and Aysha. Wonders never ceased!

At midday, Bingo returned to find Eric helping Ro to identify some of the older trucks. 'Are you tipped?' Eric asked.

'Yes. The nice agent man is sorting me out a load of workwear in cartons to go back to UK.'

'Blimey, that's a result! I'm just explaining to Ro the difference between a Volvo F88 and an F89.'

'Eric's a recovering truckaholic!' Bingo said. 'Aren't you, Eric?'

'No,' Eric said.

'What's that over there, then?'

'A Saudi Mercedes 1928, probably assembled in Jeddah, with double-drive, air-con unit on the roof and pulling one of Kamyonistan-TIR's 64-tonne tilts, which…'

'Eric!'

'What?'

'You gave the wrong answer. The answer is, "It's a lorry, Bingo." Right, let's start again. What's that yellow thing over there, Eric?'

'It's a lorry, Bingo. I wonder why Kamyonistan-TIR has routed its air-breather pipe up the nearside of the cab. You can't drive like that.'

'It must be right-hand drive, then,' Bingo suggested. 'Perhaps it was English, once. What is it, a 1928 or a 1932?'

'A 1633,' Eric said. Then he began to laugh. Bingo, realising that he'd fallen into Eric's trap, joined in.

'Nice day for a bit of truck-spotting,' Jumbo said, mischievously.

'You can shut up, for a start!' Bingo laughed.

'Look at your face!' Jumbo roared. 'All screwed up like the front of a Seddon-Atkinson that's run into the back of a pipe lorry! Come on, Ro, help me with this, will you?' He took three sheets of cardboard from behind the cab, and began to jam them behind the wipers to stop the windscreen from turning the cab into a greenhouse.

Aysha appeared, plonked Azhar in the crook of Nuri's arm and slipped away with Amoun. Bingo wandered if the two young Palestinians knew of the insipient plans for the creation of a Palestinian state ahead of plans for conflict resolution in the region. The BBC commentator had sounded hopeful on the cab radio earlier in the week.

'Come on!' Bingo said. 'Let's do a recce on foot. I want to know what the road's doing. We'll all go bankrupt sitting here.'

'Good plan,' Jumbo said, climbing down. The drivers and Ro sauntered in the direction of the main gate. A Turkish driver and the Syrian fiddler joined them.

Military earth-movers and bulldozers were already scraping out an alternative track to bypass the ruined service road. 'Good job it's dry,' Jumbo remarked. 'We'd never get out of here if it was raining.' He kicked at the rocky surface.

'It won't be very even,' Bingo said. They walked for some way along the road that led out of the transport zone. Beyond, a long queue of lorries could be seen on the narrow stretch leading from the main road, sunlight catching the trailer canopies with splashes of platinum. 'Can't go forwards or backwards,' Ro remarked, drawing one end of his *shamagh* across his mouth to keep out the dust. He felt dizzy.

'No, they can't go forwards or backwards,' Ro said to Nuri as they surveyed the mess from the top of their minaret an hour later. He still felt a little detached. A very thin cloud layer was filtering the sunlight. Soldiers guarded their vehicle compound and the site of the destroyed warehouse. The Iranian trucks were blackened skeletons, crouching in their own ashes. 'Look,' Nuri said. 'There's Mahmout climbing up his truck-wash machine. The blast must have damaged it; it's leaning over.'

'And Eric's washing his wagon by hand,' Ro laughed. His head swam. Lurking behind one of the Syrian drawbar outfits they noticed the violinist from the band. 'I reckon he's one of the secret police,' Nuri said.

'Where's he a secret policeman from? The Lost City?' Ro giggled.

'Look, Ro. Look between that green trailer and the wall.' The boys watched silently as Amoun exchanged secret kisses with Aysha. Ro looked for Azhar. Hamid was holding him, while Titania taught him English in the shade of Bingo's DAF. Ro felt spaced out. When they got to the bottom of the stairs, Ro ran for the nearest wash block and found the toilet. All was not well.

'Touch of the trots?' Titania asked. 'Better rest and drink plenty of water. No food until tomorrow.'

'He doesn't normally suffer,' Nuri mentioned, concerned. 'I think Ro's tummy got used to us a long time ago.' The drivers laughed. Precisely the same could be said for any of them.

Ro lay down on Bingo's lower bunk, leaving both doors ajar for air. 'You'll run his battery down leaving those doors open,' Eric said. 'You'd be surprised how quickly all those interior lights suck up the juice.'

'Don't worry,' Bingo said. 'They're disconnected at the door. I always do that with a "new" lorry.'

Ro listened to the sounds of chatter, of Azhar gurgling and of lorries growling across the compound. Then the afternoon call to prayer rang out and he slipped into an exhausted kind of sleep.

Titania watched Amoun and Aysha ambling towards them, brushing the backs of their hands together discreetly as they walked. 'What is it with these kids, Bingo? They don't seem to have a care in the world. You wouldn't think we've just had a rocket attack, would you? I hope we don't get another one tonight. I expect the band will play through the chaos, even if there is.'

'Band?' Bingo said abruptly. 'Shit! I forgot the piano. I should have taken it with the load this morning.'

'Did they sign for it?'

'Yes.' The unnerving sound of sirens cut through the air. Nobody could be sure whether it was an air raid warning or something mundane. Some of the factories on the zone used them to mark the end of work shifts.

'Quick! Hide under the blankets, there's a rocket attack!' Jumbo shouted. Eric cackled. Titania spread out her arms. 'I wish you lot would take this crisis more seriously,' she wailed.

Bingo's agent rode up on his moped. 'Is that an air raid warning?' Bingo asked him.

'Yes,' he replied, brightly. 'We can load you tomorrow afternoon. Usual place.'

'Good-oh! When will the exit road be ready?'

'Maybe two days.'

'Two English days, or two Syrian ones?'

'Ah! Syrian ones, of course.'

'Do you ever eat in the Restaurant Janna?' Bingo asked.

'Never. Why?'

'Just wondered,' Bingo answered nonchalantly. The light was beginning to go. He thought he could just catch the tinkle of a distant piano.

Aysha murmured sweet nothings in Amoun's ear. 'Let's take Azhar up that minaret of yours.'

'Why?'

'We could see how far he can wee!'

'He'd get altitude sickness. We'd have to make him eat coca leaves.'

'Come on, let's,' Aysha said, seductively.

'No. It's far too dangerous. Palestinian babies do not go up minarets,' Amoun said, firmly.

Ro stirred in his sleep. A fly buzzed in through one door, settled on the steering wheel boss and flew out of the other door. Ro dreamt about the little mosque garden. It was full of bright butterflies and the flowers were in bloom. Nuri was with him. All was well. Nuri climbed into the passenger seat and sat watching the gathering dusk. He missed the camels today. Seeing Mahmout scaling the damaged machine had made him wish they could have brought the camels with them. Ro reached out and took his hand. A flash lit the sky, followed immediately by a deafening roar. Ro closed his eyes. Nuri squeezed his hand.

Maghreb

A taxi pulled up outside the Seamen's Centre, tucked away down
by the railway line in Casablanca's dock area. Kevin, sixteen,
pulled his luggage from the back seat, paid and stood on the
broken pavement. Parked in the side streets were several lorries,
most of them with garment trailers bearing the names of European companies. After briefly scanning them for the familiar
vehicle belonging to his cousin, he entered the building by the
main door on the corner, leaving behind a merciless sun. Inside, it
was cool. He could hear the click of a pool table and smell the
odour of stale beer. At the bar he ordered a soft drink and sat on a
bar stool. The bar itself gave onto a large quadrangle filled with
tables and a jungle of plants with a little waterfall. Sitting at one of
the tables in the shade was Mohammed, his cousin. Kevin got up
and took his drink with him to the table. Kevin was English, born
of Moroccan parents. Every year his family returned to North
Africa to maintain links with the extended family, but this year he
had been allowed to fly out on his own. Now, he had the chance
to travel back to Europe with his cousin in the lorry. Because his
cousin belonged to that side of the family that had settled in
Holland, his first destination would be Rotterdam, then another
Dutch city, where he would stay with his other cousin, Luuk,
before returning to England.

The cousins hugged and Mohammed ordered a beer. 'I
haven't loaded yet,' he told Kevin. 'We have to be in Takkadoum
first thing in the morning.' Kevin had mixed feelings about
Mohammed. He admired him as a successful older relative, but
he disapproved of his lifestyle, starting with the consumption of
beer. For a while, they exchanged information about family
members. Kevin asked after Luuk in Holland, but did not let on
that he and Luuk had been in close contact by email for some
weeks, hatching a momentous plan.

They left the sanctuary of the Seamen's Centre with Kevin's bag. Outside in the street, the afternoon was sultry. In the distance, the 'Hassan Two' mosque floated above a smoky heat haze across the railway lines. A faded Volvo N86 with an empty flatbed trailer dozed in front of Mohammed's wagon. Kevin resisted Mohammed's attempt to take the holdall, preferring to struggle with it as he climbed into the hot cab. The less Mohammed knew about this bag the better, Kevin thought. He had wrapped the handgun well, but still he felt sure that its weight would give the game away. Mohammed fired up the Scania 143 and switched on the air conditioning. With two of them in the cab, it was going to be a hot night. When Mohammed went back into the Seamen's Centre for his shower, Kevin sat quietly and took stock. In his mind, he went through the emails he had exchanged with Luuk, reviewing their plans and reaffirming his mission.

It was clammy when they left the dockside streets of Casablanca early next day. Already, battered forklift trucks were trundling off to work in the port area. Elderly container lorries were slowly making their way along the damaged road surfaces, belching out black diesel exhaust into the morning beneath dirty palm trees. Traffic milled about them until they passed the industrial areas at 'Ain Sebaa, where the speed limit for trucks remained at a strict 40 kph. Following the coast to Mohammadia, the road plunged into a yellow mist for some time before emerging once again into sunlight. Before reaching Rabat, on the main road, Mohammed swung onto a very rough and narrow side road that took them past smoking kilns into the industrialised village of Takkadoum. This village, Mohammed told Kevin, was notorious for its ruthless and tenacious stowaways. 'Keep the doors locked, even when you're in the cab,' he said. 'And if you leave the cab, even to check the back of the trailer, lock both doors; here's my spare key. Guard it with your life!'

Mohammed reversed up a narrow street and into the tight entrance of a clothing factory, while the guardian held the tall gates open.

By mid-morning it was like a furnace in the little yard. While they were loading the hanging garments, two big youths with enormous knives scaled the outside walls. The fierce heat had made both Mohammed and the guardian less diligent than usual. While everyone's attention was on the rear of the trailer the two stowaways, or *haragas* as Moroccans called them, walked along the walls to the front end of the trailer. Climbing onto the roof, they proceeded to cut a large hole in it, very near the front. When the hole was big enough, they dropped down into the forest of plastic wrapping and pulled the outer metal flap of the trailer roof closed.

In the early afternoon, the trailer was three-quarters loaded. The loaders had made excellent time, despite the heat. Mohammed pulled out of the gateway and into the road, where he locked the cab and returned the trailer. He shut the doors, fitted a heavy clamp-lock, added two additional high-quality padlocks to the doors and taped them up with duct tape. Returning to the cab, he locked the doors on the inside and leaned out of the window. A group of menacing-looking young men, desperate to escape to Spain, were loitering with intent. Singling out the biggest member, who was carrying a stick, Mohammed called to him and handed him a fistful of dirhams. Quickly, he closed the window and drove up the narrow road. Before he had reached the end, the *haragas* were attacking the rear doors with hammers. Alas, the baksheesh hadn't worked this time. He swung out past the village mosque and increased his speed. Sweat was dripping off his face; the air-con had not yet made much of an impression on the cab.

Two lads on mopeds slewed in front of him and deliberately slowed him to a crawl. Others jumped onto the catwalk behind the cab to get at the airlines and disable the truck. Mohammed was quite accustomed to this; it happened every trip. Driving at the motorcyclists with slow, careful determination, he called their bluff and they began to move to one side. At that moment, men jumped up and hung onto the door mirrors on both sides. One banged on Kevin's window with his free fist. Swerving now to frighten those on the catwalk, Mohammed began to accelerate. One jumped, then the other. Turning right into the road that left Takkadoum, he brushed his nearside door assailant off against the hanging branches of a large tree. The other one remained until he got to the main road. There, under the watchful eye of a traffic policeman, he dropped to the ground and gave up.

'Is it always like this?' Kevin asked.

'Yes,' Mohammed replied. 'We've just got Kenitra to put on now. It's not so bad there.' The cab phone rang and Mohammed spoke for a while. 'She says the load's not ready, we'll have to load tomorrow morning. I hate parking up with half a load on.' Mohammed drove to the old road that led to Fez from Kenitra. Tucked a little way up it was a good Moroccan truck stop. It was a big, dusty place, but well guarded at night. Mohammed ordered meat from the butcher and asked for tagine. Then he went inside and ordered salad and drinks. Finally, they sat outside on the terrace and relaxed, under the impression that the load was unscathed and unaware that trouble already lurked within. That night, Mohammed slept peacefully while Kevin turned over his plans in his head.

Loading the final clothes in Kenitra proved to be slow but uneventful. By afternoon, they were bowling along the road to Tangier. Instead of taking the new motorway, they followed the old national road because Mohammed had a box of goodies to drop off with relatives who lived in Larache. The countryside was fertile, and Kevin enjoyed watching the farm workers riding donkeys, or labouring in their huge straw hats. Towards teatime they dropped into Tangier and drove through chaotic traffic down to the coast, where they followed the palm-lined seafront with its faded architectural glory and disused railway line to the port. Entering the port, Mohammed gave his details to the gate officer and parked in the export compound. Even before the engine was switched off, they were inundated with offers to wash the truck, sell them watches, run errands or change money. An agent arrived and took Mohammed's papers. There would be time to nip up to the souk, he decided. Kevin faced the port's magnificent backdrop; Tangier medina stood banked up before him, whitewashed and spiky with palms and mosques. Mohammed led him out of the port and up the narrow winding back streets and into the souks. Kevin loved this as much as anything in Morocco. He had been brought up in England but he regarded the culture of the souks as part of his heritage and in a sense, part of his identity.

Back in the port, Mohammed had the gas bottle exchanged and the cab washed, but not the trailer. He and Kevin searched the trailer chassis for new stowaways. The port was filling up with shabbily dressed youngsters looking for an opportunity to hide under the trailers as the light faded. Kevin heard a sharp knocking sound from their trailer. 'There's someone in there!' he said.

'There can't be,' Mohammed replied. He called one of the regular port kids over, who had offered to run errands earlier. 'I think there's a *haraga* inside. Nip up and have a look at the roof, will you?' The boy climbed nimbly up the back of the cab and onto the trailer roof. He returned with a bag that he'd found hanging from the underside of the metal flap covering the hole. It contained water, knives and a torch. Mohammed summoned the agent and the transport police, who opened the back and swarmed through the load in boiler suits, entering slim and exiting portly. They emerged with the two youths from Takkadoum who were only too glad to be let out, the suffocating heat in all that plastic having terrified them witless. Fortunately, they had not been in there long enough to soil the load and it was resealed.

Now the port was full of activity. All around them, Spanish fridges roared in the heat of the evening. Drivers stood in groups, drinking beer in their vests and shorts. Others sat in their cabs with their feet up on the steering wheel watching previous episodes of soap operas on tiny, flickering screens recorded for them by their wives. A heady mixture of diesel, drains and seawater odours filled the air. Every now and then, a driver would shout and pull another stowaway from under his trailer. Kevin gave a shout as he watched two youngsters climb under their trailer. 'Leave them alone,' Mohammed suggested. 'We'll flush them out on the link-span tonight.'

Later, a surly young man approached Kevin and demanded money. Kevin refused. 'We'll put drugs under your trailer, then. It's automatic prison if you're caught. Thirty years, you'd get. You'd only last five. After the first three you go mad. We'll inform the police and get the reward.'

Shaken, Kevin turned to Mohammed, who simply growled at the young man, 'You just try!'

At midnight when their paperwork and passports were

processed, they were called forward to board the ferry across the straits to Spain. On the link-span, Mohammed climbed out of his cab and, holding a lit torch, he escorted the police checker round the trailer, pointing out exactly where each stowaway was hidden. The checker had them removed and Mohammed boarded the *Ibn Batouta*.

Ibn Batouta was a fourteenth-century travel writer who knew a thing or two about long-haul transport himself. He had hailed from Tangier, and Mohammed thought that he would make a good 'patron saint' of lorry drivers; but as Kevin pointed out to him, Islam didn't really do saints and Ibn Batouta hadn't been one anyway. Exhausted, they disembarked in the Spanish port of Algeciras in the early hours and slept on the quayside until the agent knocked on the cab door for their papers. After showering, Mohammed took Kevin to one of the port bars for coffee. Their first task after clearing customs was to drive into the town to get the roof repaired. If the rain got into the load it would be ruined. So it was well past midday before they got away.

Kevin watched Spain's dramatic vistas unfold before him as they followed the Costa del Sol, where the long fingers of cypresses lazily trawled the shreds of cloud against a brilliant, glittering Mediterranean sea. It was a fierce, arid, mountainous landscape that rolled past his window. The ageing Scania growled up the long, steep mountain road from Malaga and swung east. Ten hours' hard driving took them to a truck stop north of Madrid on the 'national two.' Here they ate a good meal, which Mohammed washed down with Rioja, while Kevin clucked disapprovingly into his *agua con gaz*. When they returned to the cab, it had been broken into. Terrified, Kevin searched his bag, which he had stuffed deep into the paraphernalia of wheel braces and antifreeze containers under the lower bunk. Nothing appeared to have been taken. 'They must have been disturbed,' Mohammed said. 'Is your bag all right?'

'Yes,' Kevin said, mightily relieved. His edginess returned and he lay awake, while Mohammed snored peacefully.

The next day was hot. Using relatively minor roads, Mohammed headed across country to Pamplona and then into the Pyrenees. They rattled through whitewashed villages with geranium-filled balconies and climbed into wooded hills. The tunnel had been closed for repairs, so traffic was redirected right over the top of the mountains via the Puerto de Velate pass on the old road. Long convoys of lorries jostled in both directions on the savage climbs. At the last hairpin bend before the summit, Kevin observed the dusty wheels of the Spanish artic in front slowly revolve in powder-white sunlight as the lorries processed in low gear. Then the road dropped suddenly and they all sped up like a fairground ride. The top of the windscreen dipped beneath a distant line of blue hills. Mohammed shifted down another gear and held the exhaust-brake button down with his left foot. Warning signs flashed by and they swished round the side of the hill. Leaning on the brakes, he lost another gear and hit the exhauster again as he approached another steep descent. He downshifted a whole gear, double-declutching to ensure a clean change before plunging down yet another slope, which took them all the way down to the next hairpin bend. Mohammed passed the wheel from hand to hand as he entered the hairpin. Kevin sensed the cab reach out over the abyss before straightening up. Far below, he glimpsed huddles of terracotta roofs in a deep defile.

Ahead, the road narrowed and a Portuguese Pegaso hove into view, filling the road with its flashing windscreen and bright red presence. Mohammed slowed and hugged the rail. Dark diesel exhaust spurted from the Pegaso and its gutteral cry echoed from the rocky walls. Watching the trailer wheels in his mirrors, Mohammed accelerated hard and changed up a gear, then another, his throaty V8 shouting at the mountain. Entering another series of hairpins, Kevin watched the procession of oncoming Iberian wagons, their drivers' grizzled faces stained green, red or yellow by the transparent plastic visors that peaked their shuddering cabs.

Eventually, they reached the valley floor and followed the treacherous road that hugged the river all the way to the border at Irun. As so often happened on this route, Mohammed muddled his languages at the first French *péage* over the border, bidding the ticket attendant *'Bonjour'* upon arrival, *'Muchas gracias'* upon receipt of the ticket, and *'Ma'asalaama!'* as he released the handbrake to leave. Sometimes he would find himself saying, '*Ola, shukran,*' and '*Au revoir!*' He just couldn't predict the outcome. The last half of that day's journey took them up the long forest road to Bordeaux and up the busy RN10 to a truck stop run by an Algerian who would be sympathetic to their needs. Mohammed had a network of Algerian-run French truck stops in his head; one never knew when they would come in handy.

Their final day on the road was overcast, which made driving much more comfortable as they traversed Belgium and entered Holland. It was not until Mohammed was unloading, the next morning, that Kevin realised that his passport had disappeared. When he was questioned, Kevin remembered having left it on the dashboard after clearing customs in Algeciras. They decided that it had been stolen in Spain the night of the break-in. That night, Kevin began his second holiday, with relatives in Rotterdam.

Evacuation

Ro awoke at dawn. The muezzin's call, followed by a cockcrow accompanied by the roar of distant bulldozers, drifted in and out of his consciousness. The familiar truck-stop smell had been replaced by the stench of burning and ruin. He tried to prop himself up to reach the water bottle. Faintness nearly overcame him. His head spun and he lay back down.

At sunrise, two boys were speculating about the raid. 'They probably came back for the army trucks,' Nuri told Amoun. 'That's where the explosions came from.'

'Let's go and look,' Amoun suggested. 'Have you got the minaret key?'

'No, Ro has.' They went to Bingo's truck. Nuri quietly opened the passenger door. Titania had booked into the motel next to the restaurant the previous evening to give Ro a chance to recover. Bingo's arm hung from the upper bunk. Ro's pallid face looked distinctly unwholesome.

'Are you all right, Ro?' Nuri whispered, just loudly enough to make sure that he woke up.

'Water,' Ro murmured. Nuri opened the bottle and fed his friend. He wanted to hold the back of Ro's head up and feed him at the same time, but having only one arm he gave Ro the bottle and just held his head as steadily as he could. 'Give me the minaret key, we want to see what's happened,' Nuri said. Ro produced the key.

Amoun and Nuri picked their way through the parked wagons and stepped over bricks that had been missiles the night before. Some of the trucks bore evidence of damage, especially near the corner of the compound. 'We should be there by now,' Nuri said, puzzled. 'It's gone!' Amoun said.

'What has?'

'The minaret. It's gone.'

'But...' Nuri looked in disbelief. A tubular shard of stonework stuck thirty feet into the air. A part of his history had been destroyed.

'We could go up the minaret in the drivers' mosque,' Amoun suggested.

At first, the imam was not inclined to let them go up. He relented, however, when Nuri produced a donation to the funds. The view from this minaret was not as good as their old one had been. For one thing, the minaret was shorter, and for another, it was further away from the action. Nonetheless, they could see where the single rocket had landed: right in the middle of the military vehicle compound. The imam ushered them quickly away, not wanting to be seen spying on the army. He let them out and closed the door.

The boys went to look at progress on the track beyond the main gate. Already, the first of the stranded lorries had made their way across the stony ground, but they had become bogged down. Two Turkish trucks from the compound were reversing onto the front of the one that was stuck. They watched as the drivers attached a rigid tow bar to the bumper. It was not unusual for Middle East trailers to have a towing pin attached to the back. Linking the two reversed trucks together with a second bar, the Turks made a gallant effort to pull out the stranded wagon. Neither had double-drive, however and eventually, in spite of their diff-locks, they too became stuck. At this point, the military bulldozers moved in to assist. Eric joined the boys. Nuri told him what they'd seen from aloft. 'It's not looking good, is it, lads?' Eric sighed. In the distance they could see the musicians picking their way on foot to the main road.

An hour later, Eric met Titania and Jumbo for Turkish coffee on the veranda. 'We need to get out of this as soon as possible,' Eric said. 'It's becoming like a war zone here. They might be bent on destroying this place altogether, in which case it's only a matter of time.' Bingo joined them.

'I've just been on the Internet in my freight agent's office,' he said. 'It was Israel. They are claiming that the site is being used to accumulate Iranian weapons that threaten their state. Syria has protested and is claiming that the hostile act could be interpreted as an act of war. The international community is biting its nails. We need to go as quickly as we can. I don't mind going into Turkey empty, if necessary.'

'This is where America and Iran will wage their next proxy war, I'm afraid,' Mehmet muttered, as he collected *shay* glasses.

'You might as well get loaded, mate,' Eric said. 'The incoming trucks have blocked up the track. The Turks are bogged down and the army are pulling them out. We won't get out of here today.'

'What about you, Eric? You're going south, but the problem's the same, isn't it?'

'Yes. I don't mind about being in Syria. It's being in this little hot spot that's the problem.'

'If push comes to shove, we could always lock up the wagons and walk to the main road,' Jumbo put in.

'Then what?' Titania asked.

'Hitch into Damascus. Maybe a taxi from Homs will pass.' Jumbo sounded uncertain.

'How's Ro?' Titania said suddenly.

'Dizzy and unable to get about. I had to stick him under the trailer and hand him plastic bags this morning,' Bingo said.

'Give him lots of water. Who's with him now?'

'Nuri.'

The air was filling with drifting diesel exhaust. Several lorries had formed a short queue at the main gate. Others were starting their engines and making for the same exit. 'You'll never get out of the gate to get loaded if they block it with wagons,' Jumbo said to Bingo. Two Jordanians and a Syrian sailed past the queue and began to edge in. The English drivers stood up. 'They're either panicking or they know something that we don't,' Bingo said. 'What are you going to do, Jumbo?'

'Put the kettle on, of course!'

'What?' Titania demanded.

'Put the kettle on. There's no point in trying to play bumper cars with this lot. They'll jam everything up. No one will make any attempt at traffic control. They'll sit there revving the bollocks out of their wagons till nobody can see for smoke. Then they'll realise that the incoming trucks are doing the same on the other side of the gate and everyone will fall asleep at the wheel.'

'Seen it all before, haven't we, mate,' Eric said. Bingo nodded; he had, too. He said, 'Want another coffee?'

'No,' Jumbo said. 'If we're going to cancel, I'm having a beer.'

Titania left the trio and went to see how the patient was. This wasn't a good time to be ill. She found him sweating and restless. He drank water. Nuri was making him some broth. He'd been to the drivers' souk. 'There was almost nothing left,' Nuri told Titania. 'The drivers have been panic buying. Ro must have fresh vegetables. By the way, your gas is getting low.'

Amoun turned up, looking dejected. 'The clinic has run out of baby milk and the taxi that delivers it can't get in,' he said.

'What about the lady who fed him before?' Titania asked.

'Aysha's with her now. She's going to see if Aysha can make enough milk to feed him herself, but Aysha's milk hasn't been working properly.'

Bingo, Eric and Jumbo walked down to the great arched gateway with its imposing twin minarets. The original queue had become several queues jammed into one opening. They passed through the gate. It was clear on the other side. The police were just not letting anything through. Down at the site of the new track, most of the stranded lorries had been recovered. Eric greeted one of the Turks. He said that the drivers had been told that they would be turned round in the nearest compound and sent straight back out again. Seeing their nearly empty beer cans, he produced a pack of Turkish beer. 'Some of the drivers in the truck stop informed the Turkish consulate,' he told them. 'So now there is pressure on the military to get us out of here.'

'Do you think this lot will be cleared today?' Bingo asked.

'No,' replied the Turk. 'After that second attack last night, several drivers fled to the main road, flagged down a minibus and went into Damascus. Their vehicles are locked and no one can get hold of them.'

'That doesn't stop us getting out, though,' Jumbo observed.

Under the blazing midday sun, the three drivers walked back the way they had come. The first two Jordanians had made it under the arch and were negotiating the makeshift road. It descended a little too steeply into a big dip, then rose at an angle.

The surface had been made treacherous by the previous attempts. Trickling down the tricky track on a trailing throttle, the first bull-nosed Merc swung into the bend and immediately the unit slewed into the beginning of a jackknife. The fridge trailer was evidently heavily laden and the tractor unit bogged down. Behind it, the second lorry came to a halt. '*Mushkila kebira* – big problem. It's going to be a long day down here,' Bingo muttered.

'Let's get back to the Janna before the beer runs out!' Jumbo suggested.

As they walked, it became clear that the lorries held at the main gate had been released, but the side roads had become choked with them, where drivers had attempted short cuts. 'You'll never get down here to load up now,' Jumbo said to Bingo.

'Unless I stay and sit it out,' Bingo replied. 'The question is, do I want to load more than I want to dodge rockets?'

'And don't forget you've got a lady passenger to protect,' Eric added. 'If the main gate's clear, I think we should try and make a break for it.'

The four of them had grilled fish on the veranda and watched the compound slowly empty of trucks. Although there was no longer congestion at the gate, they knew that just beyond it, everything was jammed. Titania asked the awkward question, 'If we are forgoing a lucrative load to save our skins, who are we taking with us? We can't leave Ro behind in his condition. It would be unthinkable to leave Nuri behind. Then what about the lovebirds and their baby?' The drivers looked at each other.

'We can get Ro out of Syria, but the others haven't got papers,' Bingo said. 'But we can take them to safety. Perhaps to Homs, or even to the Turkish border.'

Nuri arrived and pulled up a chair. Eric went to get him a kebab. 'How's the patient?' Bingo asked.

'Bad,' came the reply.

'We're going try and leave in case there's another attack,' Bingo told him. 'It might be better if you both came with us to a place of safety.'

Nuri nodded and said, 'Where?'

'We don't know... Homs? The border?' Bingo suggested.

Nuri said nothing. Bingo continued, 'What about the baby, Aysha and Amoun? Do you think they might come?'

'They've already gone, I think,' Nuri said. 'Amoun is very skilful at hiding in trailers. He said that with all this chaos, no one would be checking for stowaways.'

'Has he gone on his own?'

'No. He took Aysha and the baby with lots of food and water. Aysha's making her own milk at last.'

'Oh my God!' Titania gasped. 'The baby won't survive in a trailer!'

'Let's hope they've found a tilt, then,' Bingo suggested. 'Then at least they won't suffocate.'

The DAF, the Iveco and the Volvo stood with their engines running. Ro had been netted into the lower bunk to stop him falling out. Nuri hid in the top bunk away from prying eyes. Bingo switched on his CB radio and put the lorry into gear. Eric reached the gate first, followed by Bingo then Jumbo. The queue in the service road crept slowly, stopping and starting. The afternoon was still hot and Bingo switched on the air conditioning for a while to help keep Ro's temperature down.

After about an hour, Bingo got out to look. Eric's wagon was three in front. Ahead, the trucks appeared to be turning right, into the transport zone. 'I think we're all being directed back into Kamyonistan,' Bingo said, as he climbed back into the driver's seat. 'Perhaps everything's bogged down in the dip again.' Then the queue moved up and began to crawl along the earthy track made by the bulldozers. The CB crackled and squeaked. 'Bingo! Have you got your ears on, breaker?'

'Yes, mate. I can hear you loud and clear.'

'Try and break out of the line and keep left. The Turk in front of me has gone on the wrong side of these oil drums and back onto the service road.'

'Are you following him?'

'Yes. It looks as if they've mended a narrow strip ahead. We might even get through, if no one stops us.'

'How narrow?'

'Bloody tight. Just take it slowly. Did you hear that, Jumbo?'

'Roger all that, Eric,' Jumbo's voice cut in. Bingo eased to the left and began to nose round the trailer in front. The driver clearly imagined that Bingo was trying to undertake him so he swung his tractor unit sharply to the left and hit the horn. Bingo, however, fed the steering wheel through his hands quickly and struck out across the open ground, following Eric's tracks. Jumbo was right behind. A cacophony of self-righteous air horns rang out.

Once he was on the blacktop, Bingo changed up and drove fast until he came to the ruptured surface. Just ahead, the back of Eric's trailer was making slow progress. The narrow sliver of botched road was only as wide as a lorry. In most places the edge fell several inches or more, so a misplaced wheel would be difficult to recover. Bingo watched the trailer wheels in his mirrors and slowed right down to a crawl. The CB crackled again. 'Why didn't they send all of us this way?' Jumbo grumbled.

'Because it would only take one tosser to put a wheel over the edge and block the whole thing for the rest of the day,' Eric said.

'*Roger dee*,' Jumbo replied in a mock-Yankee accent. Eric's voice came on again.

'I think the army's spotted us. They seem to be coming in from the left. The old Turk's sped up. We'd better… *bloody hell*!'

The CB went dead. Eric's tail lights flashed red and the hazards came on. The Turkish lorry in front of him nosed out to the right, fishtailed a little, and then the whole wagon leaned sharply and fell down four or five feet onto its side in a massive cloud of dust. Eric stopped. The dust began to clear. Jumbo shouted into the CB, 'Eric! Don't stop there, mate. Keep going! They'll get the driver out, look to your right.'

Several Turkish drivers had left their trucks and were running to the scene. Jumbo continued, 'We'll be here all night if we stop and we'll only block the road up for the rescuers. Just make it to the good bit, at least!'

Eric's truck moved forward. Bingo could see the army vehicles approaching the damaged section ahead. 'Go, Eric, go!' Bingo called into his microphone. 'If they get to the narrow part while we're still on it, everything will jam up.'

Eric increased his speed. Bingo changed up a gear. He leaned out of the driver's window and watched his nearside wheels run along the edge. The road seemed to go on and on. Suddenly they were among the military vehicles and the road widened. Immediately, it was narrowed again by the queue of oncoming lorries. Reduced to crawling pace, Eric eased his mirror past the first truck. This was going to take some time. 'At least we've made it. Where are we stopping?' Jumbo shouted.

'I suggest we go to the convoy stop at Homs,' Bingo suggested. 'At least it's a reasonable truck stop, and it'll be getting dark enough to hide Nuri.' Climbing out of the service road and onto the main road, Eric said, 'This is where I turn south, chaps! Doha calls. Good luck. *Bonne route!*'

'*Tareq salaama*, buddy!' Bingo answered.

'You drive careful, now!' Jumbo shouted. The remaining two lorries began to climb the mountain road as the sun set. From the rear of Eric's tilt, a pair of dismayed eyes watched them recede. Amoun had miscalculated his escape yet again.

The Golden Road to Kamyonistan

'Blimey! It's chocka in here,' Jumbo's voice announced on the CB as they swung into the huge, unlit parking area on the edge of Homs. It served as a watering hole for the official convoys of trucks traversing Syria for Turkey, Lebanon and Jordan. Bingo's headlights caught the bonnets of two ancient Berliets with pipe trailers, beyond which was a gap. 'Back off a sec, Jumbo: there are a couple of places here,' Bingo called. After peering into the space to make sure that no van or market lorry was hidden in there, Bingo positioned the DAF and reversed into the gap, leaving plenty of room for Jumbo.

Nuri was left to look after Ro and the other three went to the convoy stop building. The hall serving as a dining room was packed with animated drivers. Arabic music was playing and waiters were swerving among the tables. 'We'd better order enough for four and slip a portion out for Nuri, hadn't we?' Jumbo suggested. After Bingo had ordered, he turned to Jumbo and said, 'What are you going to do next?'

'Well, I thought I might have a haircut. There's a barber just opposite that shop out there…'

'No, mate! I meant, what are your plans? What are you going to do next?'

'Well,' Jumbo replied, hesitantly. 'I could go back to Kamyonistan in a couple of days and try to pick up your load. It should be ready by then, if the Israelis haven't blown the factory to bits.'

'That's fine by me. I'll give Istanbul a ring tomorrow and see if I can pick up a load in Izmit or somewhere.'

'What are we going to do about the boys?' Titania asked.

'If Ro picks up a bit, he'll be in a position to make a choice,' Bingo said.

'Choice?'

'Well, they may prefer to go back with Jumbo.'

'But…'

'You have to face the facts, Titania. Smuggling Nuri to England is not an option. It might have been a few years ago but not now. Customs and Immigration throughout Europe lurk on the motorways ready to pounce on anything with TIR written on it. Even if we were to succeed in running the gauntlet to the channel, we'd never get past the X-ray machines, heartbeat monitors and physical searches in the channel ports.'

'I've got Mehmet's number,' Jumbo said. 'I'll give him a ring tomorrow, when I phone the agent. He might have an idea about what's going on.' Kebab and chips with salad and *shay* arrived.

The boys were up. Ro was crouching in the driver's seat in his stockinged feet, his knees jammed against the steering wheel. He was a lot perkier. Bingo initiated a short debate about future plans. Ro was adamant that a return to Kamyonistan was preferable to being captured on the way to England. Nuri pointed out that being captured in Syria would be no picnic. 'We'll be illegal wherever we go,' Ro said.

'Or at least, one of us will,' Nuri said. 'Pity we can't go back to Nuweiba.'

'Do you think there was any connection between the police pickup running over your camel and the cleric I upset?'

'Yes. Probably.'

'You were an illegal immigrant, Ro. It was a crisis waiting to happen,' Bingo said. 'Now then, if your appetite is returning, perhaps you can share some of this grub we've brought for Nuri.'

'It's strange,' Ro said, 'but Kamyonistan feels like a sort of neutral place for us. Even here in Homs, I feel as if we've stepped out of a safe place into an insecure one.'

'Out of the frying pan into the fire!' Bingo muttered.

The following morning, on the telephone, both the agent and Mehmet were of the opinion that the attack was over. Moreover, the delay had meant that there were now two loads ready to go. Loading would be slow, however, owing to the evacuation of workers and restricted access for workers' transport.

By lunchtime it was overcast, and when they set off in the afternoon it was raining. Driving was unpleasant as visibility was poor, and the traffic was travelling much too fast for the neglected road surface and the wet conditions. Descending the Damascus road on tiptoe, they veered into the service road just as the sun came out and turned the wet mud into gold. 'The golden road to Kamyonistan!' Bingo announced on the CB.

'Roger that, mate. All I can see is the grimy arse-end of your bloody tilt,' Jumbo answered.

'You're about as romantic as a flat super-single!'

'Don't talk about super-singles, mate; I need to go against one, a bit urgent, like!'

Progress was slow, even though they had the road to themselves. Mud caked the tyres and made the going slippery. As they were empty, it was fairly easy to take a run at the dip in the track and they were quickly up the other side and back onto terra firma. Across the glistening mud Ro could see the stricken Turkish artic lying by the service road. 'What's that doing there?' Ro asked.

'Blimey!' Bingo said, turning to look at him. 'You must have been in a bad way yesterday.'

The transport zone was deserted and when, at last, they swung through the magnificent gates into Kamyonistan truck stop, they found the place almost empty but for a dozen or so vehicles belonging to the local haulier, Kamyonistan-TIR.

Even emptier, was the restaurant. Mehmet leaned on the counter rather like a village innkeeper. Bingo had never seen him so glum. 'The trade will come back quickly,' Bingo reassured him. 'Once the danger is past, they'll all come flooding back.' Evening sunlight slanted in and made radiant patches of brown and yellow among the bare furniture. Then the piano sounded. They'd all forgotten that Titania had taught music at her school. The room echoed with her lovely singing. She sang Roger Quilter's setting of the poem, 'To Daisies', by Robert Herrick. It was astonishing, not least because the piano accompaniment itself was a masterpiece of beautifully crafted counter-melodies. What made it even more astonishing was the sheer incongruousness of Titania's performance in a Syrian truck stop. Edwardian England faded with the echoes.

In the silent pause that followed, a figure appeared at the door: a boy. All eyes turned to him. He collapsed into a chair and buried his head in his arms. It was Amoun.

It transpired that a roadside check in Damascus had flushed them out. Aysha and Azhar had been returned to the orphanage. Amoun had been manhandled and turned loose. Having nowhere else to go, he'd spent his escape fund on a taxi to Kamyonistan because it had become his home and he couldn't think of anywhere else to go.

'It's probably safer for the baby in the orphanage,' Titania said encouragingly. 'Refugee babies living rough tend not to have a very long shelf life.'

Nuri put his arm round Amoun and held him. 'Just as you learn to love two good people, they get taken away from you,' Amoun sobbed. 'It isn't fair.'

Mehmet cheered them up. 'What do you want to eat? I'll need at least two waiters. My waiter, Ramazan, still hasn't returned from his annual leave in Turkey; my temporary waiter, Mahmout, is busy rebuilding his father's truck wash; so I'm going to need waiters and washers and general helpers for a while, especially when the lorries come back. I can't promise anything permanent because you're all illegal immigrants, but I'll feed you and pay you a little while I can. How about that?'

Ro punched the air and shouted, 'Yes!' The drivers smiled with relief and ordered beer while Titania played some jolly going-out-of-assembly music. Even Amoun recovered a bit when Mehmet asked him to see if there was any ice cream left in the fridge that the baby milk had been stored in.

'What's this about you upsetting a cleric in Egypt, then, Ro?' Bingo asked. Ro and Nuri gave an account of Ro's conversion and subsequent events. 'In the end, it's my body and only I decide what happens to it,' Ro said.

'So you refuse to accept the authority of "the Church" of Islam, then,' Bingo said.

'Yes.'

'So what do you recognise?'

'Its spirituality,' Ro answered.

'You're supposed to accept all of it!' Mehmet laughed. 'The trouble is, if you change your mind and decide to drop Islam, you become an apostate, and an awful lot of Muslims interpret the Hadith as demanding the death penalty for it. Others argue that those particular Hadith are "weak" and therefore unreliable, and in any case not very Islamic in spirit.'

'Interesting word, "apostate",' Bingo observed. 'Comes from a word for "runaway slave", I believe.'

'Muslims believe that everyone is born a Muslim,' Ro said.

'That's right,' Nuri put in. 'You didn't so much convert as simply rejoin.'

'But if I was born a Muslim, how can I be an apostate if I challenge it? No matter how much I refuse to conform, I'll still be a Muslim, so what's the point of worrying about apostasy? And is Islam so frail that dissenters must be killed? What's that all about?'

'Many educated Muslims would agree with you, Ro. But you must be careful,' Mehmet said. 'There are some—'

'Nutters?'

'Well, people about with strong views.'

'And un-Islamic ways of expressing them?' Titania ventured. 'It seems to me that Islam is not above criticism in Europe, but it is above criticism in the Middle East.'

'That pretty well sums a lot of things up,' Bingo laughed.

'Take Islam gently, Ro,' Nuri urged.

'Perhaps I'm just not ready for it yet.'

'One step at a time,' Nuri suggested.

The cock behind Mehmet's kitchen crowed long and loud. Standing on the low roof of an outhouse in which the three boys slept, it greeted the morning with a cry that carried beyond the walls of Kamyonistan to the ears of Hamid, who was looting. The overturned Turkish trailer was attached to a Bulgarian tractor unit. Most of the driver's belongings had been removed, but Hamid knew that drivers were apt to hide money in all sorts of strange places and he was treasure hunting. The young refugee was not disappointed, for behind a panel in the lower bunk he found a soft leather bag. A brief glance revealed documents and money, so he fled with the bag. Safe behind a disused trailer with flat tyres in the TIR parking, he crouched to assess his find. There were some bundles of notes: not a fortune, but enough to keep Hamid going for some time. There were a few identity papers, driving licences from Europe and a large number of passports. Some were French and some were Dutch but most of them were

British. All the faces were Middle Eastern. These would be no good to him, he thought. He knew that he must get rid of the passports quickly, because they would bring him trouble, especially if they were forgeries or stolen. Happily, Hamid counted and recounted the money. Then he thumbed through the passports again. That was when he found Nuri. It was not really Nuri, of course, but it might just as well have been. The face staring out of the page of the British passport in his hands looked exactly like Nuri. He looked at the date of birth and ascertained that even the age was the same.

Scrubbing the kitchen failed to be the romantic job Ro had imagined it might be. Still, he was in good company. Even Amoun was making jokes and fooling about by midday. A distant siren wailed to announce the lunch break in one of the clothing factories. Bingo and Jumbo had been on the loading bays there since breakfast time. The workers, mostly women in white overalls and head coverings, left their benches to swarm, chatting loudly, into the picnic areas where they bought drinks from the vendors and opened their packed meals. Jumbo's trailer was half full, but Bingo's hadn't been started yet.

'Keep an eye on my trailer, mate, and I'll bring a cuppa back,' Bingo said. The trailers had to be watched every single second, or the likes of Amoun would be in there, hiding among the cartons. Jumbo mopped his head. It was hot inside the trailer, which was being baked by the sun. The men in charge of loading appeared with another trolley load of cartons and Jumbo helped to throw them up to the stacker, counting each one on. Bingo returned with a welcome mug of tea. 'Shame you can't get a visa for Nuri, isn't it,' Jumbo said. 'It would be nice to get them both to Blighty and out of harm's way.'

'I don't know about "harm's way",' Bingo said. 'England is not exactly a safe place, but I know what you mean. Ro's becoming a bit of a loose cannon these days. It won't be long before he opens his mouth once too often.'

While waiting for the arrival of the next trolley, the Syrian loaders loafed against the side of the trailer and beat out rhythms on it while they sang. 'Perhaps we should be recording these,' Bingo said, wryly. 'They're probably ethnic lorry shanties waiting for some latter-day Cecil Sharp to collect them for posterity!'

'We'll be out of here tonight, with any luck,' Jumbo commented.

'*Inshallah!*' Bingo retorted. 'You know, I don't even know if Nuri has any aspirations for going to England. He's never mentioned it. I think his heart is in Sinai, really.' The chief loader returned and, with profuse apologies, told Bingo that he would have to wait until the following day to load. Jumbo, he said, would be finished by nightfall.

'You're making these damned clothes while we're loading, aren't you?' Bingo remonstrated. 'Why is it that you can never just come clean and tell us that they're not ready yet?' He had been through this conversation a hundred times before, in Morocco, in Turkey, in Romania.

'You should know better,' Jumbo said. 'If his lips were moving, he was lying.'

'Trouble is,' said Bingo, laughing, 'with that bushy moustache of his, you can never tell when his lips are moving.' Jumbo cackled. Bingo pulled his lorry off the loading bay and fastened up the empty tilt before returning to the truck stop.

Jumbo sat and stared at the dusty floor of his garment trailer. It would be a long afternoon. This was the only drawback with garments, he thought: everything took so long to load. Nuri appeared, at ground level, and smiled up at Jumbo. 'Hello, mate. Where did you spring from?' Jumbo said.

'Just thought I'd wander over for the walk and talk to Bingo. Has he gone?'

'Yes, about half an hour ago. Didn't you see him?'

'No. By the way, I noticed that you've left your roof hatch open, Jumbo. There are several kids out there I don't recognise. It might be best to close it. You know what they're like.'

'I'll give you the keys. Would you mind closing it for me,' Jumbo said.

'I can't reach up there with one arm. You need two arms to balance,' Nuri replied. 'I'll tell you what. I'll watch the back of your trailer for you while you go.' Jumbo slid down from the loading dock and made his way down the side of his wagon, whistling cheerfully.

Nuri hissed quietly and Hamid emerged from under the trailer, vaulted onto the loading dock and slipped into the load. Quickly, Nuri helped to feed him into the gap between the cartons and the roof. Then he handed up the bag of water bottles and food. Jumbo returned and thanked Nuri, who stayed for a while and chatted happily, his hand frequently straying to the little maroon booklet in his pocket.

The Kamyonistan Connection

On the veranda, a discussion about the future was underway. 'What are you going to do when Mehmet hasn't got any work for you?' asked Bingo. Ro looked vacant. Nuri looked away. 'Mahmout won't be mending the truck wash for ever, nor will Ramazan stay on holiday all his life,' Bingo said.

'Something'll turn up,' Ro muttered, unconvincingly.

'What about you, Nuri? Jumbo and I were only wondering about you this afternoon. Have you got a plan to try and get to London with Ro one day, or are you happy for him to float about in the desert with you?'

'I can go with Ro to London. That would be good,' Nuri said. Ro looked at him in amazement. Nuri had never before shown the slightest inclination to go to Britain.

'Yes, well, as we said yesterday, that just isn't going to happen with no visas and paperwork; so why waste time going on about it?' Ro said irritably.

'Don't you want to go to London, Ro? We'll go if you want.'

'What? And end up visiting you in some Greek prison or French refugee camp? Don't be so daft, Nuri.'

'Ro's right, Nuri,' Bingo said. 'This conversation is getting us nowhere.'

Titania came out, distributed *shay* and sat down. 'Lovely evening!' she murmured.

'I don't see why I should have any problems in Greece or France. There's nothing wrong with my passport, is there?' Nuri persisted.

'No, you just haven't got a visa in it,' Ro said, rolling his eyes.

'Don't need one,' Nuri said. 'It's a British passport.'

'Yes, yes. You've not been sipping *haram* beer, have you?'

'See for yourself,' Nuri said and popped the passport on the table. Still slumped indolently in his chair, Ro picked it up and thumbed through it. Suddenly, he sat up and gazed at Nuri incredulously. 'Where the hell did you get this from? You're bonkers! You'll get us all locked up!'

'It's my British passport,' Nuri protested quietly.

'But you've never told me about this. You have known me for almost two years now. Why didn't I know you had it?'

'Let's have a butcher's, Ro,' Bingo said, leaning across and taking it from Ro. He perused it silently and shook his head in disbelief. 'Nothing much wrong with that. I don't know where you got it, but it's a damned good "Mickey" passport. 'Take a look at this, Jumbo old mate.' He handed it to Jumbo, who had just entered.

'Bloody hell!' Jumbo murmured. 'You'd just better hope that passport number isn't on the "Stolen, forged and lost" register. Where did you get it from then, Kevin?' Nuri pursed his lips and shook his head.

'Does that mean we could take Nuri – sorry, *Kevin* – back in the lorry to England?' Ro asked.

'To England, yes. In the lorry, no,' Bingo answered.

'Why not?'

'For one thing, it would look too suspicious, given my itinerary. Coming from Rouen would raise eyebrows; coming from Damascus would ring alarm bells. For another, there's only one passenger seat, not three of them. Euro-police would not let us get away with that, I'm afraid.'

'We could be very bold,' Titania suggested, 'and present ourselves at the airport, pay the fine for the boys not having Syrian visas, and book ourselves out on a plane. If the passport passes the first hurdle at Damascus, the three of us should get home with no further problems.'

'Last evening she was singing "To Daisies" at the sun-dappled piano; this evening she's the criminal mastermind behind a notorious people trafficking ring from Kamyonistan!' Bingo laughed.

'What if it goes wrong?' Ro wanted to know. He'd lost Nuri once and was reluctant to risk losing him a second time.

'Ah yes,' Bingo said. 'Nuri, you're going to have to come up with a good story if that passport is on the "wanted" list.'

'I'll just tell the truth,' Nuri said simply. 'I think they'll understand. If I tell them where they can find more like this, they may
even be lenient.'

'So, what is the truth?' Bingo asked.

Nuri glanced at Jumbo and said mysteriously, 'I'll tell you next
week.'

'I'll never get used to calling you bloody Kevin!' Ro said,
sullenly.

'I'd get rid of it if I were you,' Bingo said. 'You'll fall foul of
every anti-terrorist law in the book if you get caught.'

Mehmet sat down with a glass of coffee, saying, 'No good! No
good!' He waved a hand in the direction of the television. It
flickered in the corner with the sound turned down. Figures
carrying banners were waving fists and chanting. 'That'll be the
demonstrations against those Danish cartoons depicting the
Prophet,' Bingo said. 'They've published them again to protest
against a death plot against the cartoonist. It was on the news
earlier in the week.'

'Fools!' Titania said hotly. 'Printing the cartoons just drives a
greater wedge between East and West understanding. Why can't
they just show a little sensitivity?'

'I don't agree,' Bingo said. 'The Danes should never have
offered an apology in the first place. They should have stuck to
their guns. Muslims have to learn that Western cultures don't
consider religion to be above criticism or ridicule.'

'But it's totally unnecessary to offend people just to make that
point,' Titania said.

'English people didn't take to the streets, kill each other and
have nervous breakdowns when that *Life of Brian* film came out,
and that was far worse than the cartoons!' Jumbo said.

'You have to remember that freedom of speech is not an absolute and should not be used as a means of undermining Islam,'
Mehmet put in.

'Who's to say that Islam is an absolute and freedom of speech
isn't, then?' Ro said.

'What do you mean?'

'Well, Muslims and Christians are absolutists by definition but
why should they have the monopoly? The claim that freedom of

speech is absolute is no more outrageous than the claim that God is absolute.'

'I'm not sure that you can compare those two things,' Nuri said.

'Well, I can't put my faith in a religion that's so easily offended by the slightest little thing,' Ro said.

'Ro's right about his last point' Mehmet said. 'I wish with all my heart that religious leaders would just be content to shake their disapproving beards at these things, instead of rioting and killing!'

'Well I think that there is no place for blasphemy charges in a secular society,' Bingo said. 'What if politicians behaved like spoiled teenagers every time they were criticised? We'd never make any progress, which is arguably what Islam has never made either.'

'Oh, Bingo! That's not quite fair,' Titania said. 'Look at Turkey. They have a far more pragmatic attitude to their faith there and they've made very good progress.'

'True,' Mehmet remarked. 'It was announced only recently that the Turks are looking to revise and reinterpret the Hadith in an effort to reform Islam.'

'And drag it into the twenty-first century?' Bingo asked.

'Alas, I think that it may only serve to further distance Turkey from her Islamic neighbours; but no doubt there will be many Muslims in Europe who welcome such a reformation.'

'Amen to that!' Jumbo said, standing up. 'OK chaps, I'm off. My load's tipping in Manchester on Tuesday or Wednesday week, so the earlier I make a start the better.'

Farewells completed, Jumbo returned to his Volvo and set off for the Turkish border. They watched his trailer snake over the bumps in a cloud of dust and disappear through the Islamic gate. 'Shame he couldn't wait and run back with us,' Titania said. 'I wonder what'll happen about that Dutch film. You know, the one the politician has made about the Qur'an allegedly being fascist.'

'Moderate Muslims are simply asking for European governments to consider sensible and reasonable limits on free speech when it might cause offence,' Mehmet said.

'That's a perfectly civilised expectation,' Titania commented.

'It's anything but civilised!' Bingo said. 'There's nothing sensible or reasonable about curtailing freedom of speech just because a bunch of criminals threaten violence. To demonstrate that cartoons and films portraying Islam as a religion of violence are untrue, there are Muslims who want to kill anyone who make them. The bottom line of their argument is, "Don't speak out because some of our members will do violence." In other words, the violence is always going to be someone else's fault. When are these so-called moderates going to start holding their members responsible for their own violent behaviour? Film makers and authors are not responsible for violent behaviour, only the violent are responsible for that behaviour. They make the choice to act. They make the choice not to exercise normal self-control. Why do leaders on all sides have such difficulty with this simple concept?'

'Freedom stops where other freedoms are infringed,' Titania persisted. 'Freedom of speech stops being freedom when someone else loses their freedom from ridicule or condemnation.'

'Try telling that to a man who is about to be stoned to death or hanged for bedding his best friend. Sometimes, refusal to condemn wrongdoing can amount to a denial of it,' Bingo said.

'Which is why Muslims condemn a film that condemns,' Mehmet said.

'There's a big difference between condemning something by film or ridiculing it by cartoon and going out killing and maiming people to make the point,' Bingo declared. 'This is more about violence than it is about freedom. For instance, I think it is right to condemn tyrants in the Middle East but wrong to invade their countries. By the same token, it is right to condemn offensive films and cartoons, but wrong to maim and kill for it.'

'So Christian leaders attacking Iraq is equivalent to Muslim leaders leading attacks on establishments that represent the offending films and cartoons, is it?' Titania said.

'Morally, yes. Neither Christianity nor Islam can ever be above criticism and ridicule until they renounce violence committed in their name,' Bingo replied.

'What about refusing to condemn at all?' Titania said. 'What about learning not to perceive violence as a form of attack?'

'Again, try telling that to the father of the man about to be stoned to death,' Bingo said.

A week later, Ro and Nuri were sitting in the little garden behind the drivers' mosque. Bingo and Titania had returned to England, but the boys had remained behind. Mehmet had been as good as his word and had found work for them. Amoun had pined for his 'family' and gone in search of the orphanage. In the normal run of things it might have been said that Ro and Nuri had landed back on their feet. However, Kamyonistan had not done likewise. News of the rocket attack had frightened a good deal of trade away from the transport zone. Drivers with families to support had refused to load there, and those simply passing by on the way to Damascus were taking their custom elsewhere. Some of the factories were laying off workers. Mehmet was becoming anxious. Each evening, the vast parking area saw only a scattering of lorries. Some of those drivers had never used the restaurant and continued to cook by their trailers. A strange sense of desolation was descending on Kamyonistan.

'If we get Mehmet to teach us how to be good waiters, we could get jobs anywhere,' Ro said. They were sitting on the low wall by the now derelict fountain.

'How can I ever be a good waiter with one arm?' Nuri asked, sardonically.

'You can learn to balance plates, Nuri. We could make a sort of act out of it. Then we could try and work in Damascus.'

'I'm not a circus clown. Anyway, you're forgetting that we haven't got work permits or any other kinds of permits for Damascus.'

'You're right. At least we're always invisible here, aren't we,' Ro sighed. 'Still, Mehmet will probably keep us on for as long as he can, especially now that he's realised that we know the regular drivers from our truck-washing days.' A blast of air horns announced the arrival of lorries. Their break finished, the boys returned to work.

'I've done a deal with my friend next door,' Mehmet told them later.

'The motel?'

'They aren't doing any business at all at the moment, so I've arranged for you to have a room. I have promised him that you'll be clean, tidy and respectable, so don't let me down. Also, if the place suddenly fills up or a coachload books in or something, you'll have to move out until they go.' Ro and Nuri thanked him and finished their tasks for the day. Kamyonistan was becoming 'home' again.

Friday morning was very quiet, so the boys attended the drivers' mosque for the main weekly congregational gathering. All eight of them stood shoulder to shoulder while the imam began with, '*Allahu akbar!*' When prayers were done, he delivered his 'sermon', opening with the words, 'I call today for a jihad!' He paused to let this sink in. 'I call today for a jihad for harmony: a struggle for harmony. We have in Kamyonistan, brothers from different tribes, from different countries, from different ethnic backgrounds. We have brothers with different political persuasions, with different religious traditions and even different sexual orientations. A new film is being released. I don't mean the Dutch film calling Islam 'fascist'. I'm referring to a film made by Muslims to illuminate the plight of men who love men. This film is called, *Jihad for Love*. You may feel that such a jihad flies in the face of Islam, but before we can condemn that jihad for love, we must match it with our own love for humanity. Condemning love is a serious undertaking and I suggest that instead of condemning, we declare our own jihad for harmony. Are we not all brothers in Islam? And are we not all brothers out of Islam too? We are all mujahideen: we are all 'strugglers'. Struggle requires energy. Let's not waste that energy on examining the extent to which our differences divide us. Let's instead focus on our similarities and find ways to exist side by side in harmony.

'If we cannot celebrate our differences, at least we might accept them. If your heads tell you that the film, *Jihad for Love* goes against scripture and the Hadith, listen to your hearts, brothers. If you are not prepared to look anew at the Hadith and reform it, at least listen to your hearts and remember that compassion is essential to Islam. We can start by ceasing our condemnation and replacing it first with acceptance and then with love. Why sow disharmony by criticising a man who loves another man? We can love and accept who those men are, without necessarily accepting what they do in private. If we accept them first and foremost as people, we render our jihad for harmony as potent as their jihad for love. Learn to love the next man as a human brother and you will despise him less as a Turkish secularist, a communist Jew, a homosexual Sunni, a Christian Negro, a Palestinian Bedu or an Algerian insurgent. I declare a jihad for harmony today, not as a counter-jihad to that of the film's title, but as a complement to it. With jihads for harmony and love, we move forward; with jihads for disharmony and hate, we do not. Martin Luther King, in his own struggle, suggested that if we don't live together as brothers we die together as fools.'

There was some irony in the imam having delivered his somewhat unorthodox 'sermon', not to hundreds of thousands at Mecca but to eight worshippers, seven of whom did not speak Syrian Arabic well enough to understand the full meaning. There was Ro, who did not get any of it; Nuri, who gleaned fragments; two Turkish drivers, over whose heads went nearly every word; a couple of lapsed insurgents newly escaped from Iraq, whose Maghrebi Arabic was not up to grasping its import; and an Iraqi Kurdish refugee who worked at Kamyonistan-TIR as a sweeper, whose first language was Kurdish. In addition there was a young student imam who understood every word, but whose hard-line Islamic politics told him that the imam himself should be usurped at the earliest opportunity.

'Communication is everything,' Mehmet told the imam later, when he dropped in for coffee. 'You were probably preaching to the converted, none of whom understood you. Now you've ended up communicating with the single destructive element in your ranks, the student. He may stir up trouble, but I shouldn't worry too much because not many wannabe imams can stomach working in this outpost! Keep up the good work. I'll see that the young foreigner understands what you were getting at. Now then: more coffee? Will you stay for a spot of lunch?'

Fair Play

Jumbo was no Francophile, but he was a discerning traveller nonetheless. Over the years he had developed a nose for seeking out good watering holes down the old transport routes of *la belle France*. In fact, he had an encyclopaedic knowledge of that durable network of truck stops known to the French as Les Routiers. Having reached the last leg before Calais, Jumbo made a detour from the motorway and took to *les routes nationales* in search of one last good meal before he returned to the gastronomic catastrophe of England's notorious rip-off motorway service areas. The trusty Volvo rumbled serenely into the verdant depths of rural France, where chickens scuttled among the buttercups and where each village seemed to be in that permanent state of dilapidation that Jumbo called 'unspoilt'. Roadside ditches were filled with creamy drifts of cow parsley and a delicious air of natural abundance prevailed. He was not disappointed as he tucked into an excellent, reasonably priced four-course meal and quaffed *vin rouge* at a table of affable Spanish and French drivers.

The following morning, he checked his wheels and lights and examined the locks and seals on the trailer. He checked the sides for any sign of stowaway damage and set off into a climate of cloudy spells. Going down one of the long slopes typical of French motorways, a car drew alongside sounding its horn. Jumbo looked at his speedometer and noticed he was doing four kph over the speed limit. Irritated, he sounded his air horns in the hopes that the 'jobsworth' would accelerate and go. However, as Jumbo found so often happened these days, the driver was a 'road rager' and he swung his saloon into Jumbo's path and hit the brakes. Jumbo had always regarded this particular type of intimidation as one of the stupidest, because a forty-tonner could not be stopped quickly. Once upon a time he might have braked or swerved, thus endangering other road users, but now he drove serenely on. The car braked heavily and accelerated repeatedly, each time narrowly missing collision.

Jumbo hoped the police were watching from some vantage point. He had a policy for this eventuality. If the car driver miscalculated his manoeuvre so that Jumbo ran into the car, then Jumbo would continue driving. If he were subsequently caught by the police and charged with failing to stop for an accident, he would insist that it hadn't been an accident but a deliberate act of aggression from which common sense suggested that he should flee. The driver eventually lost his nerve when he realised that Jumbo appeared not to have bothered to knock off his cruise control.

Descending into the port from the end of the motorway at Calais, he was pleasantly surprised to find that the queues were relatively short. Soon, he was ushered into a shed for the first set of checks. He switched off, climbed out and greeted the officials. They attached sensors to the trailer chassis and watched the monitor. Satisfied that no hearts were beating within, they wished Jumbo a good day, and he moved on to the ticket booths. The girl issuing his ticket told him that he would just make the next boat if he went directly to the ferry. He passed through the next bank of booths where he was required to show his passport to the British immigration authorities. Next, a British team screened his trailer once more. Because Jumbo's was a garment trailer and not a tilt, it was not necessary to use the carbon dioxide probes. They asked Jumbo questions about his load and wanted to know what checks he had personally made, before letting him go. The team of French checkers employed by the ferry company had just completed their last internal trailer check when Jumbo arrived in the holding lane. The lane was empty. He was clearly the last vehicle to board and the checkers waved him onto the ferry without checking Jumbo's trailer doors.

There was always a strange familiarity about the drivers' dining room on a cross-Channel ferry after a Middle East trip, Jumbo thought. Sipping his post-prandial tea and watching the sunlight sparkle brilliantly among the waves, he was aware that the same crew members cheerfully went about their daily tasks, for all the world as if time had stood still, awaiting Jumbo's return. Nowadays, it was less cosy. Only a handful of years previously, the dining room would have enjoyed waiter service and a large number of the drivers would have been British, many of them known to Jumbo. Jumbo's view was that now that Britain's apathetic attitude to road transport had priced its own lorries off the international trail, the room was always full of foreign drivers, largely from newly adopted EU countries, whose subsidised trucks were brimmed with cheap diesel. He had long ago lost the will to get excited about this sort of thing. After all, soon he'd be back out again and heading south, even if he was the only British driver aboard.

The ferry docked and Jumbo went down onto the loading deck. As usual, his lorry was missing. He had never been able to work out why, after so many years on this job, it was possible to mislay a fully freighted wagon in a cross-Channel ferry. It happened every time. Jumbo always imagined that other truckers must instinctively know where they had left their vehicles, but as he ducked under trailers dripping with loops of snow chains, he met hollow-eyed drivers in padded lumber shirts who quite obviously had not the remotest idea where their lorries were. He began to fantasise that he hadn't brought one aboard at all. Once in his cab, he stared at the back of the trailer in front, looking forward to that triumphal part of his journey in which the faithful Volvo would bellow up the steeply rising curl of Jubilee Way into the ivory cliffs of Dover.

The Middle-Easter dipped his clutch, engaged a low gear, released the air brake and followed the line into daylight. Driving down from the link-span Jumbo made his way along the network of elevated roadways and into the final checking area. A uniformed man wearing a hi-viz vest stopped him and pointed to the X-ray machine. Never mind, Jumbo thought, at least I managed to escape the internal check in Calais.

Jumbo stood in the waiting room while the machine scanned his wagon. 'Would you like to come with me, sir? We think you may have a bit of a problem.'

The voice broke into Jumbo's reverie. The stench that hit them when they opened the back doors informed them that all was not well. Jumbo thought of the massive insurance claim against his rejected load.

An ambulance was called and Jumbo was asked if he recognised the body. With nothing to lose by saying otherwise, Jumbo told them that the lad was called Hamid and that as far as he knew, he had been a Palestinian refugee. 'And you say you think he got in while you were loading in Syria?'

'Correct,' Jumbo said.

'You will, of course, be aware that this carries a fixed penalty of two grand per head of illegal immigrants,' the official said.

'I've already told you that I watched that load on myself. No one got in while I was standing there,' Jumbo said, wearily.

'Well, I doubt if that explanation will do you any good, I'm afraid.'

'This'll bankrupt me. Where am I going to find two grand? What's more, if I'm fined, the insurance company will no doubt consider me guilty and nullify the cover. Then I'll have to sell the truck, if you haven't already impounded it, plus my house to pay for all this nonsense.'

'Nonsense?'

'Yes! If my stowaway had still been alive, you'd be asking him what it means to be British and teaching him about English fair play. You lot are finding me guilty until proved innocent. I thought fair play was about being innocent until proved guilty!'

'This regulation has worked well, nonetheless.'

'How can injustice be called "working well"? Have you any idea what it's like trying to load in the Middle East with all sorts of murky characters hanging about at the arse-end of your wagon?'

'You don't have to lecture me about the Middle East, driver, I was a helicopter pilot in the Second Gulf War,' the official said, just a little self-righteously for Jumbo's liking.

'All right, Air Wolf, keep your hair on, mate. Anyway, there wasn't a Second Gulf War, it was an invasion; another example of British fair play, no doubt.'

'OK. Let's get back to nuts and bolts. Your truck will be impounded. We will try to ensure that your court case is brought as soon as possible.'

'I'm telling you now,' Jumbo growled angrily, '*I am innocent*!

Therefore I will not be paying any sort of fine. I will go to prison rather than pay a single farthing – and that's final.'

Bingo and Titania were in what remained of Londra-Camp TIR parking at Yeni Bosna in Istanbul. An air leak had grounded them for a day. As it was sunny and Titania was with him, Bingo asked the resident taxi driver to run them down to the district of Kumkapi, where they sat on a terrace belonging to one of the fish restaurants overlooking the Sea of Mamara. He ordered some Turkish white wine and they settled in for a leisurely lunch. 'An ideal spot for the Paradise Club!' Titania laughed. 'How's your notion of paradise located in childhood holding up these days?'

'Very well,' Bingo replied. 'I've been trying to make up a new word for the concept. A new word that loses the baggage of "child spirit" and "inner child", but still conveys the concept of continuing childness; the concept of a certain kind of light that we carry with us; a spark of vitality, spontaneity and joy within. I thought of using the word *Im*. Then I reflected that in all references to the interior presence of the Christ Child or the divine child within, we might easily substitute the word *Im* for Christ Child, thus stripping the references of religious connotation.'

'Why do that?'

'To purify it. To remove the deity filter from it.'

'It occurs to me that our yearning for paradise, having located it in childhood on the one hand, and our instant recognition of our past selves in the antics of children on the other hand, form two parts of the same mechanism,' Titania observed.

'Explain.'

'It seems to me that the delight we take in observing childhood in action would appear to be a component of the human condition worldwide. That is to say that humans value the presence of children very highly. You once said that children appear to exist almost in a different dimension as if they were another race. Little children, especially, appear in this way to be more like goblins, fairies, pixies and elves simply because adults don't do all the things in shops and streets that children regard as entirely normal – flopping down, standing on their heads, pulling faces, sudden running, spontaneous jumping, exuberant skipping, hopping, spinning, balancing and twisting. Perhaps we have evolved to treasure, to value these childhood traits and to find them worth protecting in exactly the same way that we appear to have evolved to find children attractive and worth protecting for the survival of the species. Might our perception of paradise in childhood be a vital component of this protective mechanism? Maybe we recognise not only our precious elven past selves in children, but also recognise the state in which we last knew paradise. In this way the whole concept of paradise might be part of our evolutionary survival kit.'

'Yes, I like it. The more we kick the childhood-paradise thing around, the more it loses its metaphysical mystique. The hardest part, it seems, is reactivating the child within adults. I can't understand why it is so difficult to convince adults that they still have the programme within them that once enabled innocent playfulness and incalculable quantities of sweetness; or why it is so difficult to dislodge the crusty sleep of adult drudgery from their eyes and return their turbid souls to quicksilver.'

'When you find out, just let me know and we'll rule the world!' Titania laughed.

That evening they headed north into Greece and by the next afternoon they were following the delightful coast road that dipped and swooped through Xanthi and Kavala, affording glimpses of idyllic bays with pastel reflections of villages in still waters, framed with rocks and cypresses. After Thessaloniki, Bingo's air system began to play up again, so instead of going over the mountains south of Lamia, he headed for Harry's Truck Stop in Athens.

Dutch Courage

With his head down into the slanting rain, Kevin turned the corner where a street organ was churning out a cheery arrangement of '*Geef mij maar Amsterdam!*' and crossed the canal by a bridge. Even though it was only early afternoon, lights were on in the shops and cafés in the little square beyond. Kevin pushed open the door of the café and tucked his Arab-pattern scarf down into his jacket, out of sight. Luuk was waiting in the corner.

'Sorry I'm late. I caught the wrong tram,' Kevin said. The youth shook hands with Luuk, who had stood up to greet him.

'That shouldn't mess up the plan, inshallah,' Luuk said. He was the same age as Kevin. Luuk ordered coffee for himself and a fizzy drink for his cousin. 'Any news of your passport yet?' Luuk asked, in a low voice.

'No. It's three weeks now. I don't like going to the consulate all the time because it draws attention to me. The whole point of my coming here was to carry out this mission against the infidel film maker and slip home unsuspected. Now I'll have to stay here until the consulate can replace it. It's raising my profile.'

'Don't worry, we'll keep you as anonymous as we can. So, you've been staying with Mohammed's lot in Rotterdam for well over a fortnight. You must tell me how everyone is, later. Have you got the…?'

'*Ssh!* Yes. It's in this carrier bag of onions.'

'We'll go to my aunt's house tonight. From there, we can climb onto the roof and go to the back of the building. It overlooks the school where the film maker's friend's daughter studies.'

'Good. Are you sure you know what she looks like?'

'You can't miss her. She's really beautiful. It's a waste, really,' Luuk said.

'But it's in a good cause. We must "take her out", and then the film maker will have to repent.'

'Inshallah,' Luuk prompted.

'Inshallah.'

Outside, the rain was easing off a little, so the youths paid and left. Leaning against the wall outside was Luuk's bicycle. He pushed the bike while they walked. Kevin filled him in on the family news. At one point they stopped by a brilliantly lit clothes shop to drool over the latest designs, their sense of materialism briefly at variance with their sense of fundamentalism. Rainwater spilled from the guttering high above them and Kevin pulled his *shamagh* over his head. Seeing Luuk's momentary look of alarm, he hastily pulled the hood of his anorak over the *shamagh*.

Luuk's aunt lived in a narrow cobbled street lined with saplings. Parking the bike in a hallway, he pushed open the inner door and they ascended a steep staircase. It was dark at the top. Luuk led the way into an apartment and switched the light on. An impeccably kept room greeted them. It couldn't have been more Dutch, Kevin thought; but then this particular aunt was Dutch through and through. Her convenient absence had made this plan possible. A large table was covered with a green chenille tablecloth over which lay an embroidered linen one. On the table a Delft china bowl of fruit presided over dishes of cold meats and sliced cheeses, left for them by the kind, unsuspecting aunt. Net curtains were gathered at the window and every available surface was festooned with trailing pot plants.

'Come on,' Luuk said. 'I'll get you into the mood for this, while we have something to eat.' He went over to the television and taking a package from a bag of onions, he posted a DVD into the machine. While Kevin munched his stick bread, alternating it with mouthfuls of cheese with pickled gherkins, he watched the anti-Western propaganda that would help him to justify the act of murder that he was contemplating. Luuk had downloaded the material from a website. Like Kevin, he had become a terror junkie, the Internet having poisoned his mind no less than heroin might have.

After their 'fix', they prayed for compassion on the day of judgement. The night was long. Neither slept well. In the early hours, they got up and went over and over the elaborate plans that Kevin had made at the back of his old maths exercise book from school. They watched the DVD again and Luuk told Kevin that he could keep it.

Morning dawned grey and squally. As the school hour approached, the boys climbed onto the roof and crawled on their bellies to a vantage point above the school playground. Several teenagers were huddled against the dry side of the wall, clutching brilliantly coloured umbrellas.

'That's their car – the silver one,' Luuk hissed, pointing down into the road. Three girls got out and slammed the doors. For a while, they chatted by the gate.

'Which one is it?' Kevin demanded.

'I can't tell yet. They're all too covered up with raincoats.' After a while, the girls moved into the yard and caught the full force of the wind. The hoods of two of the girls blew back, one of them letting loose a stream of auburn hair. 'That one, Kevin! The hair, look.'

Kevin moved to a parapet and crouched against the stonework. Luuk continually scanned the roof and neighbouring windows to make sure that they were unobserved. A tall girl on the other side of the playground shouted in greeting and called the trio over.

'Quick now, before it's too late!' Luuk shouted. Kevin lifted the handgun and took aim. Luuk urged, 'Don't let them get out of range!'

Kevin imagined the glorious place his name would occupy on the Internet and he squeezed the trigger. The noise was horrendous. Startled, everyone in the playground looked round. Some people in the street looked up. Kevin fired again. The girls began to run. He began to shoot in quick succession. One bullet chipped the brickwork above the school gate. It seemed to Kevin that the gun lacked range. To Luuk it seemed that Kevin had never used a gun before. A taxi driver gave a shout and pointed at the roof.

'He's seen us!' Kevin said. He was beginning to wish that he had not worn such a bright yellow shirt that morning.

Luuk peered over the parapet and urged, 'We've still got time to kill her, shoot again!' More people had gathered near the taxi driver, and they too began to point or to yell into mobile phones.

'Quick, let's go! *Yallah!*' Kevin shouted. The boys panicked and fled.

They did not stop running until they were safely under the bridge over the canal. They could already hear sirens. 'The taxi driver saw us. What if they search the house?' Kevin said.

'They won't know it was us. Only my aunt lives there, and she's in Leiden,' Luuk assured him. 'By the way, I hope you didn't leave that DVD in the telly.'

'Shit, yes. But that still won't identify us.'

'Well, I hope you've got your exercise book with you then,' Luuk said. Kevin shook his head. 'What?' Luuk shouted. 'You left all the evidence in the apartment? Oh, no! It even has your name on it!'

'I couldn't think of everything. You were supposed to be the support team,' Kevin said, lamely.

'Oh yes! While the master crack shot sniper was accomplishing his mission successfully, I was supposed to go round removing all the evidence, was I?'

'Yes.'

'Not exactly the sharpest little crayon in the box, are you, Kevin? Where's the gun?'

'On the settee.'

Kevin thought about going straight home to escape from this nightmare, until he remembered that he'd have to go to the passport office in the consulate first. He had painted himself into a corner. His delusions of grandeur evaporated and he turned to Luuk. Luuk had gone. Kevin climbed up onto the road and shouted, 'Hey! Luuk!'

'You're on your own now, mate!' Luuk called, before setting off at a run.

Kevin walked into the centre and found a café. After buying a coffee, he sat down to try and think straight. Taking a sheaf of visiting cards and receipts with names and phone numbers scribbled on them out of his pocket, he noticed that his hands were shaking badly. One particular name jumped out at him: a good contact over the border in Belgium. With any luck, they would hide him. He paid and went out into the wet, cobbled street to look for Belgium.

After about half an hour, he found himself in an industrial area. Passing a cold store, he noticed a British-registered lorry pulling off a loading bay with its doors pinned back. He saw his chance to return to the UK without his passport. Running to the rear of the trailer, he scrambled into the back and began to climb the pallets. He heard a shout and felt the driver pulling him down. Kevin protested and said he'd get down.

'Oh! So you speak English,' the driver said. 'Are you completely brainless? I saw you in my mirrors. This trailer is refrigerated. Can't you hear the motor roaring away? The thermostat is set for minus twenty-five. You'd probably be dead before we even got to Calais!'

Two turnings further on, Kevin entered Industriestraat, which was cobbled. In the second yard he came to, a skeletal trailer was standing on its own with a short shipping container on it. The back doors were open and a forklift truck was pushing shrink-wrapped pallets into the back. When the forklift went off to fetch the next pallet, Kevin investigated. He read the labels that were stuck to the shrink wrap. They had an address in Birmingham printed on them. After the forklift had pushed another pallet in, a loader inside the trailer appeared. Lighting a cigarette, he climbed out and went behind a wall to finish smoking it. Kevin leapt in and climbed to the front of the load. He had beaten the passport problem. 'I'll give Luuk "Not the sharpest little crayon in the box",' he muttered.

An hour later the rear doors slammed shut. Inside, it was pitch black. Five hours after that, a tractor unit backed onto the trailer and began its journey to the docks. Kevin was beginning to wish he had planned more carefully. He was desperately thirsty and the air was becoming stuffy. Trying to be as brave as the Moroccan *haragas*, he pretended he was escaping to Spain from Tangier. He thought about how the Moroccans escaped. They used machetes and tools to cut their way out of garment trailers or simply slashed their way out of curtain-siders. Kevin wished he had a heavy knife.

Then he remembered what Mohammed had said about never stowing away in a container because the sides were too strong and no fresh air could get in. Mohammed had also mentioned that containers had a nasty habit of remaining in stacks for weeks on end until the goods inside them were required. 'Warehousing on the cheap', he'd called it. Horror stories of containers falling off ships in foul weather, freezing in the cold and roasting in the sun began to haunt him. He lost all track of time. At one point, he awoke to a terrible heat. The sun outside was warming the thinning air in the little gap between the load and the container roof to an unbearable temperature. Already too weak to panic, Kevin prayed and fell unconscious.

Identity Crisis

Towards the end of the following month, Mehmet detected a marked change in the general ethos of Kamyonistan. In the restaurant, his young members of staff were settling in well. Ramazan had not returned from Ankara, and Mahmout had become too absorbed in his work at the truck wash to show much interest in waiting at tables. Not that there were any trucks to wash; the flow of traffic had been reduced to a trickle. Most of Kamyonistan's vendors and hangers-on had one by one moved away, either as a result of the rocket attacks or because of Kamyonistan's changing fortunes. The greatest changes, however, lay in the bigger picture. In their haste to restore Kamyonistan to the status of innocuous transport zone, the military had sealed off the target areas, placed them under skeleton guard and withdrawn to camps further up the mountain. Several premises, including clothing factories, had shut down – either temporarily or permanently.

The vacuum created by this set of circumstances was, inevitably, filled with unwelcome forces. At first, the boys had reported the presence of surly youths and unruly young men in Kamyonistan. Then drivers began to complain of intimidation by a new breed of aggressive stowaways who used threats of violence instead of skill. The occasional visits by the local police soon revealed that they were fast learning to regard Kamyonistan as a no-go area. Over a glass of Turkish raki, one local officer complained to Mehmet that organised criminal gangs were occupying some of the abandoned premises, and that their members were insurgents with combat experience who had escaped from war-torn Iraq. One night, a particularly vicious attack on a Turkish driver for his wallet was enough to frighten all but the bravest of truckers away.

That was the same night that Eric, having picked up another

'seller' for Doha, was crossing the Bosphorus that divided Europe and Asia in Istanbul. He was piloting a Renault Magnum with a load for Saudi Arabia. This would be his final 'seller', he'd decided. He preferred to write articles. Three days later he rolled into Kamyonistan. At first, he thought the place was closed. 'It's like a ghost town here!' he remarked to Mehmet, when he ordered his beer.

'Before you drink that,' said Mehmet, 'I should bring your wagon close up to the front here. It won't be safe parked out in the middle. It's a wonder they haven't nicked that palm tree you've parked under.'

'They?'

'The mercenaries – the insurgents from Iraq.' Mehmet apprised Eric of recent events.

Nuri brought the beer in and joyful greetings were exchanged. Ro emerged and they all sat down. 'We daren't go out any more,' Ro said miserably. 'Mehmet's had to get a dog. He's out at the back. He doesn't even like us, let alone intruders. It used to be dangerous when we lived here last time, but this is far worse.'

'You should think about moving on, then,' Eric advised.

'Heard any news of Bingo or Titania?' Ro asked.

'No, but Jumbo's been banged up.'

'Prison? Why?'

'Illegal immigrant in his trailer. Apparently, he climbed in at the factory here in Kamyonistan. Jumbo refused to pay the fine.'

'What happened to the stowaway?'

'Dead. Jumbo said it was that tall kid, Hamid,' Eric told them. Ro and Nuri looked in horror at one another.

'Do they think Jumbo hid him in the trailer?' Ro asked.

'Of course! That's English justice nowadays.'

'But he didn't hide him, I did,' Nuri said, candidly. Ro and Nuri told Eric about the deal Nuri had done with Hamid in order to obtain the passport with his likeness staring out of the important page. Eric was astonished by this revelation and found it necessary to drink more beer before deciding on his next move.

Eric gazed levelly at the boy sitting opposite. 'If you went to England, you could testify. Jumbo might just stand a chance of getting a fair hearing.'

'Don't we need Hamid to corroborate?' Ro said.

'Yes, but he's dead.'

'What if they won't take Nuri's word?' Ro asked.

'That passport of his will provide a fair bit of evidence,' Eric suggested.

'But they'll just think Nuri stole it himself.'

'That's tricky. Hey, Mehmet, whatever happened to the driver of that truck that fell over on the service road last month?'

'He was Bulgarian. As far as I know he's in Damascus prison for drug running. They found a consignment on his wagon,' Mehmet said. Nuri shuddered and thought of the stash of stolen passports he'd hidden behind the locked door to the stump of their minaret.

'If push comes to shove, maybe we can get the British end to do a little probing in Damascus. I think it's worth a try. 'First though, I need to get the trailer electrics looked at. Being a "seller" this trip, I haven't got any tools with me.'

Ro rode with him as he steered the Magnum round to the workshops. Several sinister-looking characters made grudging way for them when they passed through the gate. In the absence of daily repair work from traffic passing through, the teams of mechanics were busy rebuilding old tractor units from the chassis up. The half-finished shells of several Scania 141s, 'New Generation' Mercs and an Iveco Turbostar stood in various states of restoration.

'In Syria, old trucks never die!' Eric laughed. Sipping the *shay* offered to them while the work was being done, Eric outlined his rescue plan for Jumbo.

The following morning, Eric found a seedy little secure TIR parking near the airport. Mehmet had strongly advised him not to leave his truck in Kamyonistan. Their flight had been booked from Mehmet's office. Cheap European clothes had been found for the boys in the local market from where they had caught a taxi to the airport. The three of them were equally nervous as they approached the passport control. An official made a good deal of fuss about the boys' missing visas, and they had to go from window to window just to pay the fine and obtain visas that could then be franked and cancelled. It occurred to Eric that the visa crisis had possibly distracted attention away from the passport itself. They would never know, of course.

The flight itself felt strange to all of them: for Eric because of the strangeness of his mission; for Ro because he was apprehensive about returning to England; and for Nuri because he had never been in an aeroplane before. In addition, Hamid's death and Jumbo's imprisonment tormented Nuri's conscience. Knowing that the worst was to come, the three passengers said little.

At Heathrow, their fears were confirmed at the first hurdle. When Nuri presented his passport he sparked a major alert and several officers appeared in order to take him away. Eric and Ro had to make quite a lot of noise before anyone would let them accompany Nuri. Even then, they were escorted at a distance.

'So let's get this right, then,' the official summed up, two hours later. 'This dead stowaway, Hamid, allegedly removed passports from an overturned Bulgarian truck in Syria. Upon identifying a passport photo that bore a strong resemblance to Nuri, he agreed to let Nuri have the passport in return for Nuri's help to hide him in Mr Gaugewick's truck.'

'Who?' Ro said.

'Jumbo,' Eric hissed.

'Nuri maintains that he distracted Mr Gaugewick in order to achieve this and that Mr Gaugewick was unaware of this event. So far so good?'

'*Yes,*' Eric and Ro said together.

'Both these boys believe that the Bulgarian driver might be able to corroborate their account of the stolen passport, and Nuri knows where the rest are hidden. You may or may not be aware that the rightful owner of this passport was wanted for an assassination attempt in Holland that is being treated as an act of terrorism,' the official went on. 'Earlier this week, he turned up in a container in Dartford docks. His parents identified him. They thought he was enjoying an innocent holiday with relatives.'

'Poor devils! I blame the Internet.'

'He was held responsible for his own behaviour. The Internet cannot be held responsible for the choices he made,' the official said, curtly.

'Was he really Nuri's double?' Ro asked.

'No. Whereas the camera never lies, it often fails to reveal the whole truth. In this case, a combination of light, angle, expression and who knows what else contrived to create a plausible twin for Nuri out of Kevin's picture.'

'Do we have a case, then? To free Jumbo, I mean,' Eric asked, hopefully.

'Putting aside Nuri's serious attempt to deceive British Immigration and your own attempt to aid and abet him, sir, yes. If his stash of passports is wanted by Intelligence for anti-terrorist reasons, Nuri's information may well be taken into consideration. Don't hold your breath yet, though. We'll see what they come up with in Damascus. Now then, have you any questions?'

'Yes,' Nuri said, stoutly, 'I wish to request asylum.' Eric buried his head in his hands and Ro closed his eyes.

To their amazement, the official asked, 'Do you want me to record this request?'

'Yes please,' Nuri replied. 'Hasn't my sense of fair play been an indication that I understand the nature of Britishness?'

Eric chuckled. Then Ro laughed and slipped his arm through Nuri's. For once in his life, Nuri was not laughing. He was deadly serious.

At the highest road pass in Morocco, an artic was pulling out of the little rest area at Tizi 'n Tichka. Under a blazing sun, Mohammed aimed his Scania south, taking the steep, tight bends in low gear. He faced an afternoon slowly descending the High Atlas mountain roads. Later, after creeping through sleepy villages with brightly painted, square minarets, he began to encounter the rocky beginning of the Sahara Desert. That evening, his delivery of supplies to a film studio in Ouarzazate completed, he strolled into the pleasant desert town for a phonecard. It was some days since he had spoken to his family because he had not bought a card when he entered Tangier. News of Kevin's death and Luuk's arrest shocked and upset him. He was angry that Kevin had taken the gun to Europe in his lorry, risking imprisonment for both of them; he was distraught that his cousin was dead; he was distressed that the cancer of religious violence that was killing Islam was now gnawing at his own family; and he was despairing that fine boys like Kevin and Luuk were falling foul of this terrorism drug just as surely as the fine boys of Manchester were destroying themselves with alcohol or heroin. His family in Morocco, England and Holland comprised a network of supportive, loving souls who wished no one any harm.

Mohammed found it difficult to make any sense of his world. He thought about drinking the beer that the film crew had given to him an hour earlier. Instead, he went to the mosque. Had he been a man of creative prayer, he might have demanded to know what the hell God thought he was up to, but Mohammed knew only how to recite the set pieces by rote. It was mechanical, like praying by numbers. After his prostrations, he felt about as spiritual as a broken half-shaft. Mohammed wanted to stop the rot that was poisoning his culture, but he did not know where to begin. Somewhere, in an English lorry park, there would be a similarly distressed driver who did not know where to begin to stop the cancer of mindless, alcohol-fuelled attacks on members of his own family. Like this English driver, he felt powerless to do anything. So he drank the beer anyway and spent a hot and sleepless night in the desert, wondering if the West would take refuge from alcohol in Islam while the East took refuge from Islam in alcohol.

A Long Way from Kamyonistan

Eric, who had flown back to Damascus to pick up his 'seller' and continue his journey east, parked in the desert in front of the customs buildings at Abu Samra, the Qatar side of the Saudi border at Selwa. He brushed the fine, grey, dusty sand from his mobile phone but he could not get a signal. Reviewing his journey, he reflected that he had been lucky that his spell in Britain had not dislocated it too badly. Even his TIR carnet had not been compromised. After an initial false start for repairs in Damascus, he had crossed Jordan and the Saudi desert to a gas field between Hofuf and Harad, where he had tipped his load of pipe elbows before proceeding to Qatar. Eric had loaded the pipes in Scotland, where pipes were specially constructed to withstand the corrosive nature of the gas produced in this part of the Gulf.

A Qatari driver called to him in greeting and offered him coffee. He spoke excellent English and introduced himself as Amir. Amir was driving a very battered-looking right-hand drive Foden that still had half the name of a previous English operator signwritten to the roof board. It was, clearly, a past 'seller'. 'How much do you think you'll sell your truck for in Doha?' Amir wanted to know, after their second cup.

'Depends,' Eric said, vaguely.

'Let me look,' Amir said. So Eric showed him inside the cab. 'Aha! Left-hand drive,' Amir exclaimed with delight. 'Excellent! My truck is no good now: the Qatari government doesn't like the steering wheel on the wrong side any more. I'm looking for a newer truck. How many horses?'

'500,' Eric replied.

'I could pull a heavy bulldozer with that,' Amir said, enthusiastically.

Eric arranged to meet him in a hotel in Doha long frequented by British drivers on the Middle East run. The following day, they ran together up the hundred or so kilometres of desert road to Doha. Leaving their trailers outside the customs compound, they drove solo into the city and parked in the hotel car park. Eric had all but sold his Magnum.

Meanwhile, it seemed to Mehmet that Kamyonistan's vicissitudes were of no further interest to the outside world. The outside world having stayed away, he busied himself by redecorating the dining area. After several attempted break-ins by the lawless mob that rampaged among the deserted factories, he managed to persuade Mahmout to lodge with him. The attempted break-ins continued, however, and one morning they went out to find that the guard dog's throat had been slit. That was the final straw. Mehmet decided that he would board the place up and work in Damascus until Kamyonistan became safe again.

Fate intervened after the first boards had already been nailed across the windows. Two rival gangs had got into the area sealed off by the military. A shoot-out ensued during which one group of gangsters detonated, perhaps inadvertently, a large stockpile of ammunition. The explosion gave the false impression that the Israelis were rocketing the zone once more. In consequence, most of them fled into the mountains. This explosion in turn, attracted the attention of the military leaders, who returned to keep an eye on the place.

It was from these officers that Mehmet received the news about the ammunition going off, along with reassurances that things would improve. One by one the factories reopened. Amoun returned with Aysha and little Azhar to work in the restaurant. Lorries began to arrive in greater numbers each evening, and before long the place was beginning to feel like Kamyonistan again. Mehmet received a visit one morning from the personnel manager at Kamyonistan-TIR. 'Have you still got those two camel lads with you?' he asked.

'They've gone to Britain, but I don't know how long for,' Mehmet replied. 'Why?'

'Well, we're opening our own agency here in the freight agents' building next to the truck stop, and we're looking for intelligent runners who can speak English. Nobody will come out from Damascus since the attack. If your two lads show up, I could get them work permits.'

Far away in a greenish land, other events were unfolding. During Jumbo's court proceedings and Nuri's initial interviews, Ro and Nuri stayed with Titania. Hers was a large, pleasant house with a garden. As a temporary measure, Bingo stayed there too. One evening, they sat at the dining table with the smell of lilacs coming through the open windows and discussed the possible options if Nuri was permitted to stay in the country. Questions concerning the possibility of going to school and of finding work were explored and revisited. Bingo and Titania even talked about making room for Bingo in the house so that Nuri would have a ready-made family to move in with.

'That music is very evocative, Titania. What is it?' Bingo asked.

'It's Delius's setting of the poem you so audaciously butchered in the Janna that night you ran off with Mahmout!' Titania laughed.

'Oh yes, Flecker: "The Golden Road to Samarkand",' Bingo said.

'I like it,' Ro said.

'If you listen carefully, you can hear the camel bells, as the caravan makes its way eastward,' Titania said. Nuri told her that he could hear them and that the music reminded him of his lost camels. 'Delius also wrote a piece called "A Walk in a Paradise Garden". Do you want to hear it?'

Ro thought of their paradise garden in Kamyonistan and nodded. It seemed to Nuri that Bingo and Titania were made for each other despite Bingo's preferences. He said so.

'We'll see,' was Titania's smiling reply.

Once Jumbo had been released and his truck restored to him, all efforts were made to ensure that Nuri's bid for asylum received a fair hearing. Another fortnight passed. They visited a school, the beach, some pubs and four restaurants. To Ro it all felt a little unreal; to Nuri it all seemed new and strange. Bingo serviced his lorry and took on some local container work to keep the wheels turning. Titania was preparing for a concert.

Sitting on the hard wooden chairs in Canterbury cathedral, the boys let huge waves of sound wash over them. This was particularly apposite for a number of reasons. Firstly, the waves of sound were being created by a local choral society rehearsing Vaughan Williams's *Sea Symphony*, and the cavernous building was doing interesting things with the dramatic music. Secondly, Nuri, whose head was resting on Ro's shoulder, was learning to let life, the universe and everything wash over him. Thirdly, a possible journey across the sea was imminent, Nuri's application for asylum having begun to founder in its early stages. Plans were not proceeding with much promise. Not that he would catch more than a glimpse of the sea from his flight to Egypt, but the sense of journeying was ever present in the music. When the choir made its entries, a glorious noise took hold of the cathedral's interior. The music ebbed and flowed with its own tides while Ro's thoughts and emotions ebbed and flowed entirely out of sync with it. Ro was less inclined to let life's vicissitudes wash over him. He was more resistant to what, to Nuri, appeared to be the natural order of things. Nothing, to Ro, was ordained by fate.

Nuri, who was unaccustomed to this strange music, found it difficult to follow. He singled out Titania, who was standing in the soprano section watching the conductor attentively. The music stopped abruptly and the conductor's voice echoed eerily, though the boys could not hear his words. Somewhere, a cello was being retuned. Eventually, Ro suggested that they move on. Outside, the rain came down in dully sparkling lines, making the great trees in the precincts seem greener. They huddled under the Christchurch gate and gazed across a jumble of empty plastic furniture in the Butter Market. A lone, oblivious busker performed to an audience of passing umbrellas, his guitar hopelessly out of tune. Window-shopping was the only option left that they could think of.

The sea returned to their lives that afternoon because Titania took them out for a meal on the coast, where they could watch the water while they ate. To begin with, none of them mentioned Nuri's possible departure. Instead, they made plans for things to do while he remained. By coffee time, however, Ro could contain himself no longer and when Titania went to sort out the bill, he said, 'I'm going with you to Egypt. If you can't stay I won't stay either.'

'What's the point?' Nuri said.

'There doesn't have to be a point,' Ro said. 'Anyway, I want to make sure that you are all right. My tourist visa would last for a month, and in that time I could help you to settle. Maybe we can get your camel back. If your family fetches you from Saudi, at least I can be with you until they come.'

Once again, Nuri was faced with making the choice between his family and a life in which he would not be forced to live a lie. When his family had gone to Saudi Arabia, he had remained behind in Egypt on this single issue, part of which was his desire to be with Ro. Ideally, he would have loved to live with Ro in Sinai as a camel driver in the bosom of his family. Ro had observed bitterly that Saudi's culture paid only lip service to family values, while banishing 'dishonoured' daughters and gay sons. Titania had reminded the boys that much work remained to be done in order to achieve mutual cultural understanding.

'You'll probably be sent home, if they think that you're trying to work again,' Nuri said, glumly.

'Not if I keep my head down,' Ro responded. Nuri shook his head.

'They know about you now. They won't let go. Anyway, who's going to pay for your flight?'

'What if we hide you here, then?'

'That'll only prolong the agony,' Nuri said. 'I'd be caught in the end. Bingo said that Britain is no longer a country to hide in.'

'I just don't know where we can go, where we can be together!' Ro said. He sounded exasperated. It was all to do with passports and visas. Ro continued, 'What we need is a place that doesn't seem to notice us. Somewhere where we can be invisible.'

'Like Kamyonistan,' Nuri said.

'Yes, that's right. A bit like Kamyonis…' Ro looked at Nuri and their eyes met.

Titania returned. 'When is Bingo doing another Middle East trip, Titania?' Ro asked.

'I don't think there's anything going down there at the moment,' she replied. 'He said something about "groupage" to Spain.'

'What about Jumbo and Eric?'

'I don't know. You'll have to ask them. Why?'

'Just wondered.'

That evening, while Titania was performing in the cathedral, Bingo took the boys down to the yard. Several staples had come adrift on his tilt trailer and he wanted to rivet them back into place. It was quiet and the air was fresh and pleasant. Squatting with his back against a trailer wheel, Ro turned the drink can in his hand. 'Do lots of people try and stow away on lorries going abroad, Bingo?'

'Good heavens, no! They don't even bother to check out-bound lorries in the ports,' Bingo said. 'Except on the Channel tunnel of course, but then they're looking for terrorists.'

'What about after that?' Ro asked.

'You could probably get all the way to the Middle East,' Bingo laughed. 'But nobody would ever stow away going south, they're all too busy coming the other way!'

'Do you know if Eric's taking another seller down?'

'Ask him yourself. He's joining us for Nuri's final hearing, if he gets back in time.'

'Which way does he go down?' Ro persisted.

'He used Italy and Greece last time, but he might use Hungary, Romania and Bulgaria, like we used to. It should be easier now that most of the eastern bloc is in the EU. Mind you, he did say that the trip he's just done would be his last, so don't hold your breath.'

'If we do have to make a break for it, we'll have to pick a tilt. We've seen two boys killed and I don't intend to join them,' Nuri told Ro later.

'We're not duffers,' Ro replied. 'We ought to prepare a small backpack with water, tins and tools.'

'And a torch.'

'If Eric isn't going and if Jumbo's taking a garment box and if Bingo's doing Spain, we could try a Turkish trailer, then find a truck going to Syria from Turkey.'

'Too risky. What if the Turk's going to Russia? What if the Turks catch us and imprison us or ill-treat us? What if we can't find a truck going on to Syria? We need one that's going all the way.'

'But that can take over a week! We can't spend that long cooped up in the space between the load and the roof,' Ro protested.

'How else do you think we're going to get there?'

'Have you any suggestions?'

'By going in a truck whose driver knows us,' Nuri said.

'What do you mean?' Ro asked.

'Do you remember that Jordanian driver, Wahid? He took us to Kamyonistan from Nuweiba and we weren't too afraid because we knew he was looking out for us.'

'I see. So if we talk to Jumbo or someone, he'll let us out for air and grub when it's safe, and lock us back in again for each stage of the journey,' Ro murmured. 'But Jumbo's just had one scare. If we're caught he'll lose his livelihood. He'll never agree to this plan.'

'He doesn't have to. We'll stow away and once the journey has started, we'll bang on the side to let him know we're in the trailer. After that he'll be cross but he'll still help us,' Nuri suggested.

'But what if he doesn't hear us? What if an immigration officer hears us instead? We won't be able to tell when it is safe.'

'We'll be able to feel the sea crossing. After that we'll wait for one driving shift and then bang on the sides. We should have arrived in a truck stop or a lay-by.'

'Or we could talk to Bingo and see if he'll just agree to take us.'

'Let's just see how my hearing goes first,' Nuri said.

Eventually the time of reckoning arrived. It was a beautiful spring day. Late blossom speckled the pavements with pink. Jumbo and Bingo wore suits for Nuri's final asylum hearing. Titania, who had been advised by Bingo to appear less Bohemian lest she be mistaken for a new-age do-gooder, was wearing one of her 'parent evening' outfits. The charcoal suit was topped with her straw hat, which lessened its austerity somewhat. Ro and Nuri were in smart casual wear, and both looked sleek and well scrubbed. They sat outside in a pavement café and drank tea.

'I think we've been a pretty formidable team, so far,' Titania said.

'I think Nuri's got a reasonable chance,' Jumbo added.

'I thought you played the safe-to-be-gay card to good effect at the last session, Bingo. And I suppose, in reality, it's true that if he were refused asylum he would have to return to his family in Saudi Arabia, where he could face persecution. With only one arm he couldn't support himself in Egypt, and they wouldn't give Ro a work permit to wash trucks. I'm sure all that helped, even if it didn't tip the balance by itself,' Titania remarked.

'It's just a pity that they sounded so unoptimistic,' Bingo replied.

A breeze stirred the tablecloths. In the distance, they could see Eric making his way towards them. 'Shame baby Azhar couldn't be here,' Ro said.

'I think we'll just have to let baby Azhar stew in his own juice for now, don't you?' Titania replied.

'He'll do that wherever he is,' Ro giggled. Nuri laughed.

Eric joined them, looking very dapper in a good suit. 'Made it back, then!' Bingo commented.

'Half the bloody truck was missing when I got down there,' Eric said. 'It cost me loads of baksheesh to get everything spirited back again.'

'Get a good price for it?' Jumbo asked.

'Better than I expected, so I can't really grumble. Here, do you want to hear a heart-warming story?'

'Go on then, Eric,' Bingo encouraged.

'Before leaving Damascus, I had to return to Kamyonistan because my heater was blowing out red-hot air no matter what I did with the switches, and I didn't fancy crossing the desert in Saudi with it.'

'That sounds very heart-warming,' Bingo laughed.

'Hang on – I haven't finished yet! I took it to one of the workshops but they were busy and suggested that I took it round to Kamyonistan-TIR. They've got their own workshops. Well, standing in their yard were those twelve Iranian Eurotrakkers, minus their Tehran number plates. Half of them were already in Kamyonistan-TIR's colours and one even had one of those fancy Syrian-style camel bars fitted.'

'I don't get that,' Ro interrupted. 'We saw all the Iranian trucks burnt out by the bombed warehouse, didn't we, Nuri.'

'Yes. We could see them from our minaret.'

'Our ex-minaret!' Ro corrected.

'That was just the loaded trailers,' Eric said.

'What about the drivers, then?' Nuri asked.

'Defected.'

'Catch me doing that,' Nuri said, dryly.

'They'd already uncoupled and moved the units before the rocket attack, fully intending to defect,' Eric continued.

'And in doing so, they must have saved their own lives,' Bingo put in.

'Exactly! One of the drivers showed me a unit that was awaiting its new livery, and guess what? They've all got Twin Splitters!'

'Oh no! Stop him someone. Did you ask them for a job?'

'The Eurotrakkers will be good replacements for Kamyonistan-TIR's ageing Mercs,' Eric said.

'Well, fancy defecting from one police state to another!' Bingo said. 'I suppose they'll get away with it if Iran doesn't look too closely at its satellite pictures.'

'The driver I spoke to cited the intolerable level of religious policing as their chief reason for defection,' Eric said.

'Aha! Back to the subject of the authority of the "Church", eh, Ro?' Bingo said.

Eric sat back, brushed his jacket with his hands and straightened his tie. 'Your tie's got camels on!' Nuri exclaimed.

'To bring you luck,' Eric said. Nuri was touched. He supposed that he would always be a cameleer in Eric's eyes.

'Well, if the British justice system treats you as fairly as it did me in the end, we'll be home and dry by teatime!' Jumbo said.

'If Nuri stays and you both go to school,' Eric said, enthusiastically, 'you could do Arabic and Middle East Studies. My nephew seems to think it's a subject in its own right.'

'I'm not sure if that's just at degree level,' Titania said. 'But it would be worth looking into, wouldn't it? You could both do something with your Arabic for sure.'

'Nuri would walk it!' Eric said.

'There's a Spanish proverb which says that you have as many lives as the number of languages you speak,' Titania said.

'Always make the most of languages,' Bingo added. 'In this work you really do see the necessity for it.'

'You don't want to go into transport, that's for sure! It seems to get worse by the month here. What if he can't stay? What then?' Eric asked. Nobody answered. Nuri sighed and fiddled with his shirt hem.

Titania broke the silence by turning to Nuri and asking, 'Are you sure that this is what you want?'

'*Suel gharib!*' Nuri answered, with a frown.

'What does that mean?'

'Strange question,' Ro translated.

'No stranger than asking for asylum,' Titania said. 'The trouble with asking for something is that you may actually receive it. That's why I asked you if this is what you really want. That goes for you too, Ro.'

'What do I really want? We need to go in the drivers' mosque again to sit and ponder the question, like we did that time when we wanted to know about paradise. Do you remember?' Ro said.

'I just want to live and work with Ro in peace, if that's not too much to ask!' Nuri said, turning the small Iraqi coin in his pocket. 'But you've never known me to lose hope, have you?'

Ro nearly asked, 'Live and work where?' but he was not sure of the answer himself, so he remained silent. Nuri wondered, briefly, if the coin could be traded for the price of an airfare. A phone in Bingo's pocket beeped and he took it out to read the text message. It was from his UK freight forwarder and it said: <We have load 4 Syria. Ru intrstd? Ring soonest.>

Across the road, a huge weeping willow hung above rich, green grass. Delighted cries of children playing, echoed from somewhere behind it. A church clock chimed the hour. The little group fell quiet. In their own ways, each of them was thinking of Kamyonistan. It seemed strange that such a tiny place, so far south from their table on the pavement, had become so significant in their lives.

'I wonder if Kamyonistan will survive,' Jumbo said.

'In the absence of Kamyonistan's physical presence, there is still Kamyonistan,' Eric said.

'How do you mean?' Titania asked.

'Even with Kamyonistan's removal from the mountains of Syria – even with its closure and its ceased existence as a geographical place – it continues as an abstract,' Eric said.

'I see what you mean,' Bingo said. 'It's a concept. More than that, for us Kamyonistan is a construct. It is a place in our heads.'

'Yes,' Eric agreed. 'Not only for those of us in the Paradise Club here, but for the whole community of Kamyonistan it is a sort of archetypal Middle East truck stop.'

'It's a way of life!' Ro put in. 'If you close your eyes in another truck stop, you can still be in Kamyonistan in your head.'

'Precisely,' Eric said.

'Do you mean that Kamyonistan is a feeling, an attitude, a collection of experiences we take with us into the next truck stop?' Titania asked.

'Yes. It's a sort of blueprint we carry in our minds to help us to recognise what we want and expect from a good stopping place.'

'I know what you mean,' Titania said. 'It's the same with schools. I once left a school in which I had been happy and successful. The school was closing down and was due to reopen as a mixed community college the following September. In the final assembly, I was presented with leaving gifts. When I addressed the girls, I held up a house brick and when I told them I was presenting it to them, they laughed, of course. Then I showed them the hollow part and mentioned that it was called a "frog". There was more laughter. Then I showed them that I had chalked the name of the school on the front of the brick. After that I asked them to close their eyes and remember all the very best things that they had loved about the school that was closing, and suggested that they mentally visualise placing those precious things in the frog of the brick. Next, I turned the brick round to show that I'd chalked the name of the new school on the other side. I told them that I was leaving them the brick so that they could take all the best of the old school with them into the new one, and that in September the brick would act as a reminder.'

'Were they sad?'

'No. I think they just found it instructive. It was members of staff who did the crying!'

'So we take the spirit of Kamyonistan with us wherever we go,' Ro said.

'Yes,' Eric replied. 'In psychological terms I suppose it could be said that we project our notion of the Kamyonistan ideal onto other locations. In this way we could apply the principle to European truck stops or to those floating truck stops known as "freight ferries".'

'A sort of metaphysical lorry park, then,' said Bingo, laughing. 'This isn't the Paradise Club anymore, it's the Kamyonistan Club! Greater Kamyonistan is that "other country" now.'

'Ro said that two years ago,' Nuri said. They looked at him in surprise.

'Did he?' Bingo asked.

'Don't you remember his dream about Kamyonistan being paradise? In the dream, though, he couldn't reach it,' Nuri said. 'Sura 13;35 in the Qur'an says, "This is the Paradise which the righteous have been promised; it is watered by running streams; eternal are its fruits and eternal are its shades." It's supposed to refer to Damascus. Apparently the Prophet, peace be upon him, stood in our mountains and looked down upon the oasis of gardens that is now the city, but he was reluctant to enter that earthly paradise in case it diverted him from his quest for the more ethereal one.'

Now, if Ro and Nuri closed their eyes, they could just smell the *shisha* smoke and diesel; they could just hear the call to prayer; and they could just see the procession of lorries dragging their clouds of dust under the distant palms as the boys led their camels home at twilight. Their camel era in Kamyonistan now lay beyond the great divide, in boyhood. Those days would never return, and they knew this. Yet they had returned to Kamyonistan at a new level, with different energies. Kamyonistan itself did not necessarily belong to the unreachable past. Potentially, it belonged to a rosy future filled with opportunity. Boyhood may have slipped behind them, but the optimism of youth would remain their stoutest ally for a long time yet.

Almost as if she had read their minds, Titania raised her tea-cup and murmured, 'To Kamyonistan.' They all reached for their cups and replied, 'To Kamyonistan!'

Printed in Great Britain
by Amazon

81007228R00068